JOHNNY BOO

"TWINKLE POWER"

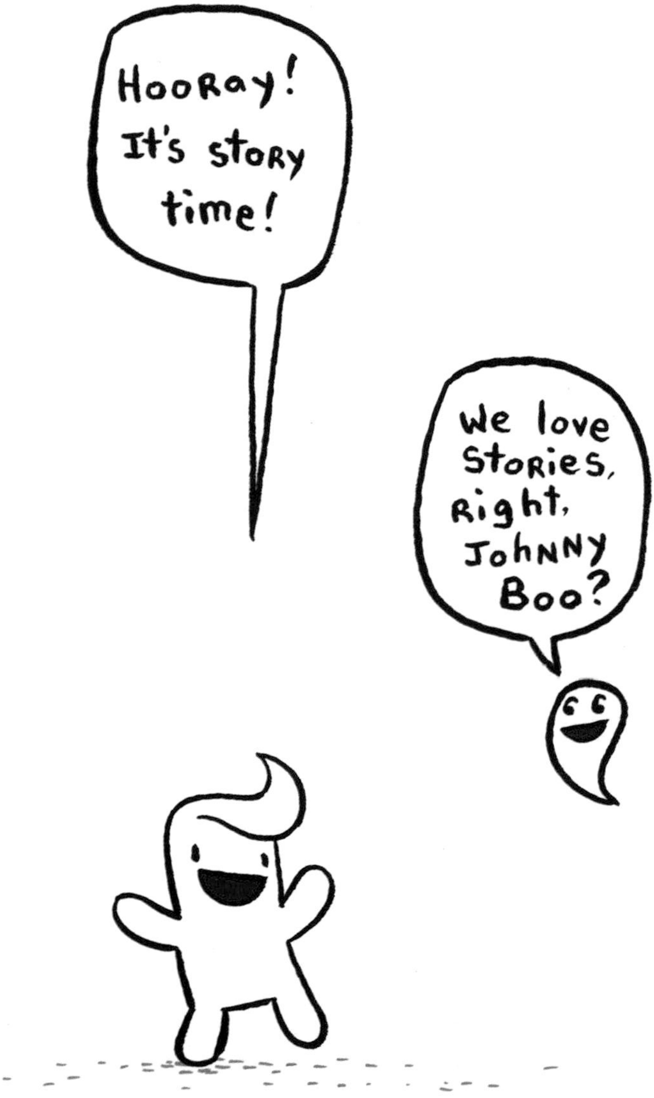
Hooray! It's story time!
We love stories, right, Johnny Boo?

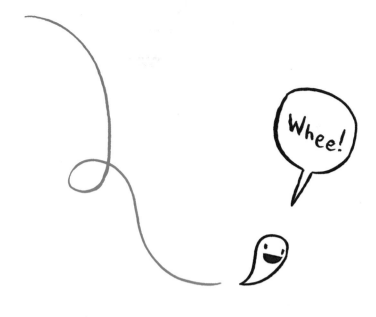

FOR MY BOYS,
Eli & Oliver

Johnny Boo: Twinkle Power © 2008 James Kochalka.

Published by Top Shelf Productions, PO Box 1282, Marietta, GA 30061-1282, USA.
Top Shelf Productions is an imprint of IDW Publishing, a division of Idea and
Design Works, LLC. Offices: 2765 Truxtun Rd, San Diego, CA 92106. Top Shelf
Productions®, the Top Shelf logo, Idea and Design Works®, and the IDW logo
are registered trademarks of Idea and Design Works, LLC. All Rights Reserved.
With the exception of small excerpts of artwork used for review purposes, none
of the contents of this publication may be reprinted without the permission of
IDW Publishing. IDW Publishing does not read or accept unsolicited submissions
of ideas, stories, or artwork.

Editor-in-Chief: Chris Staros.

Visit our online catalog at www.topshelfcomix.com.

Printed in Korea.

ISBN 978-1-60309-015-5

20   19   18   17   6   5   4   3

CHAPTER ONE:

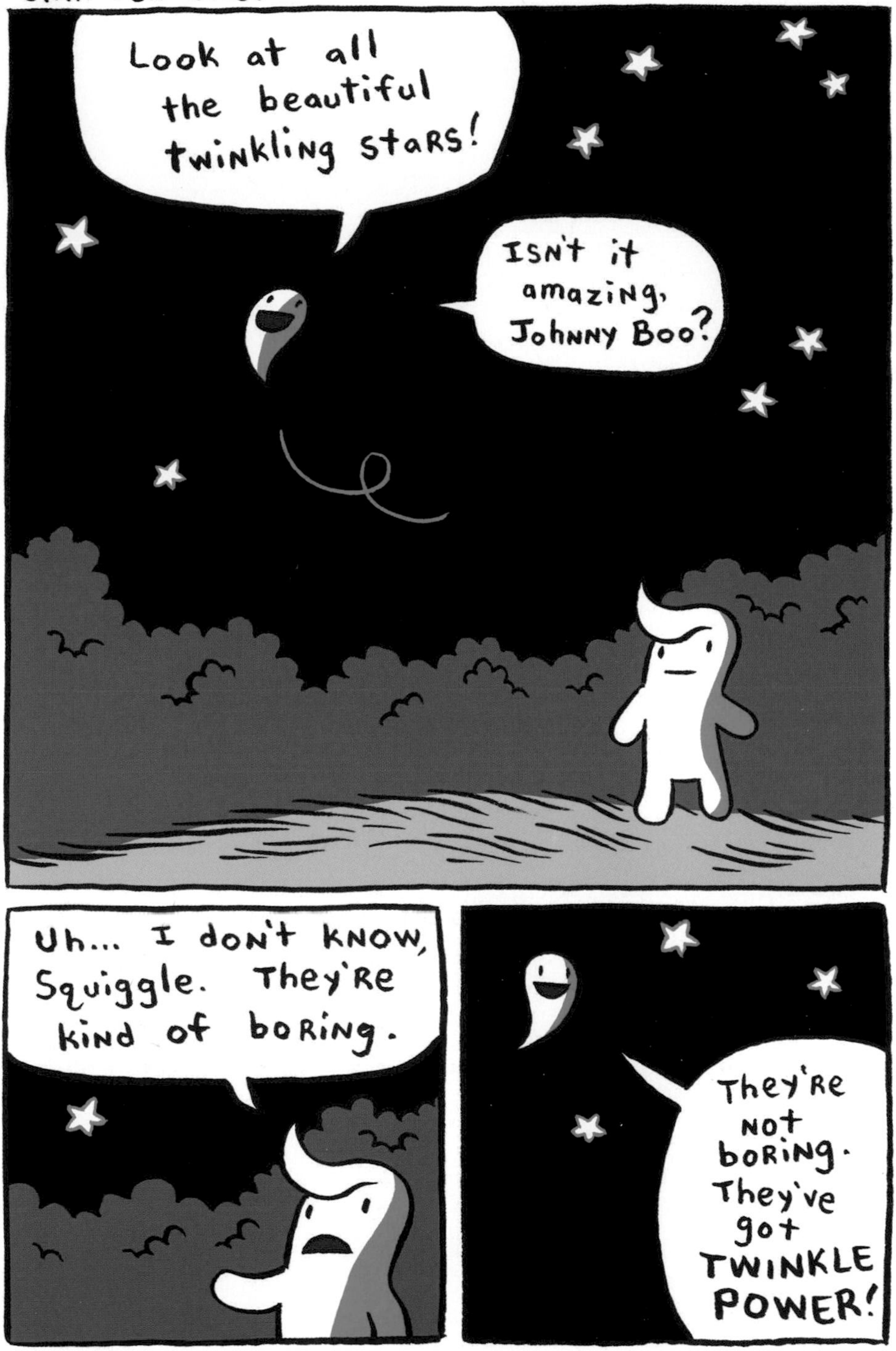
Look at all the beautiful twinkling stars!
Isn't it amazing, Johnny Boo?
Uh... I don't know, Squiggle. They're kind of boring.
They're not boring. They've got TWINKLE POWER!

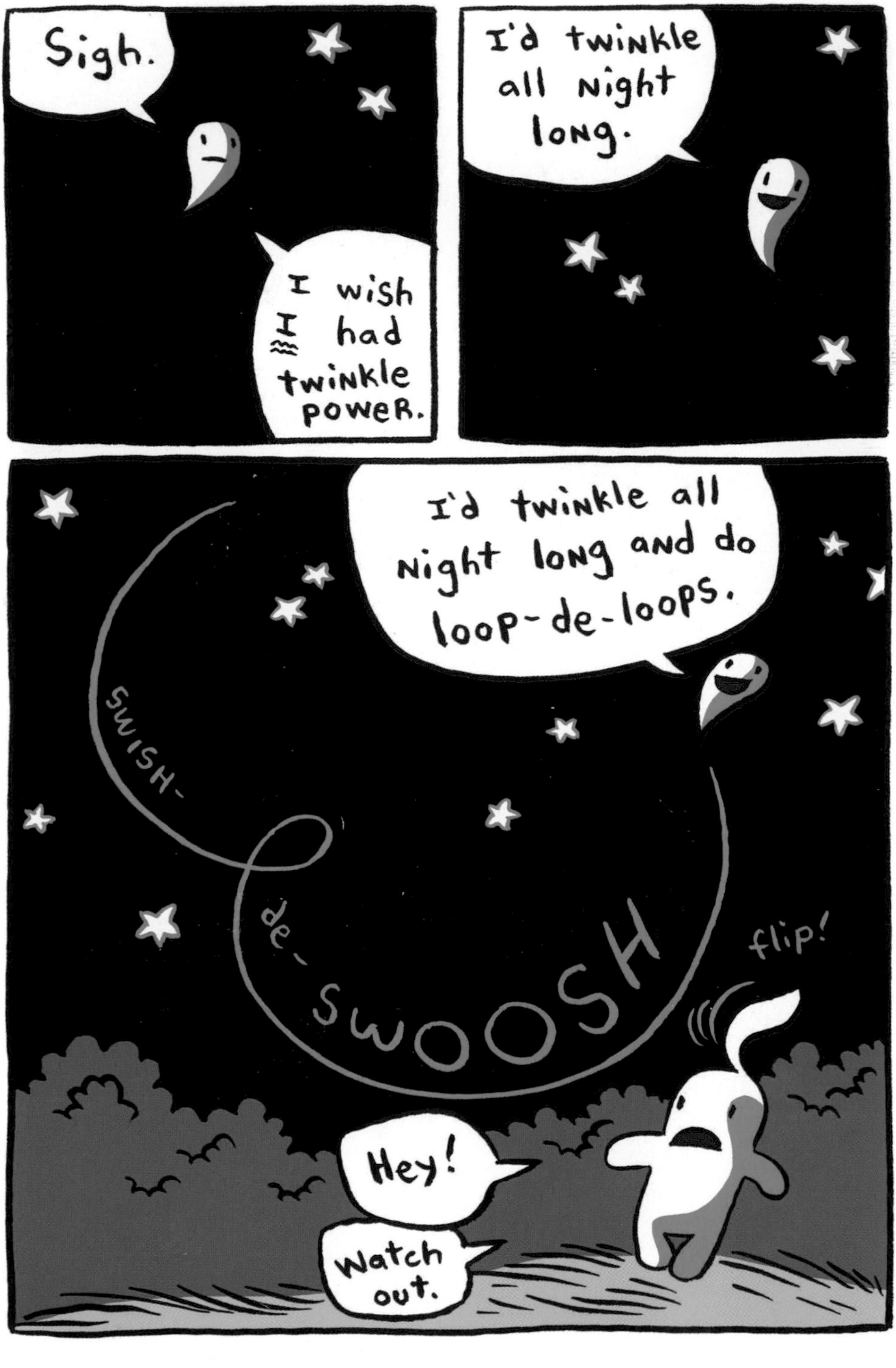
Sigh.
I wish I had twinkle power.
I'd twinkle all night long.
I'd twinkle all night long and do loop-de-loops.
SWISH-
de-
SWOOOSH
flip!
Hey!
Watch out.

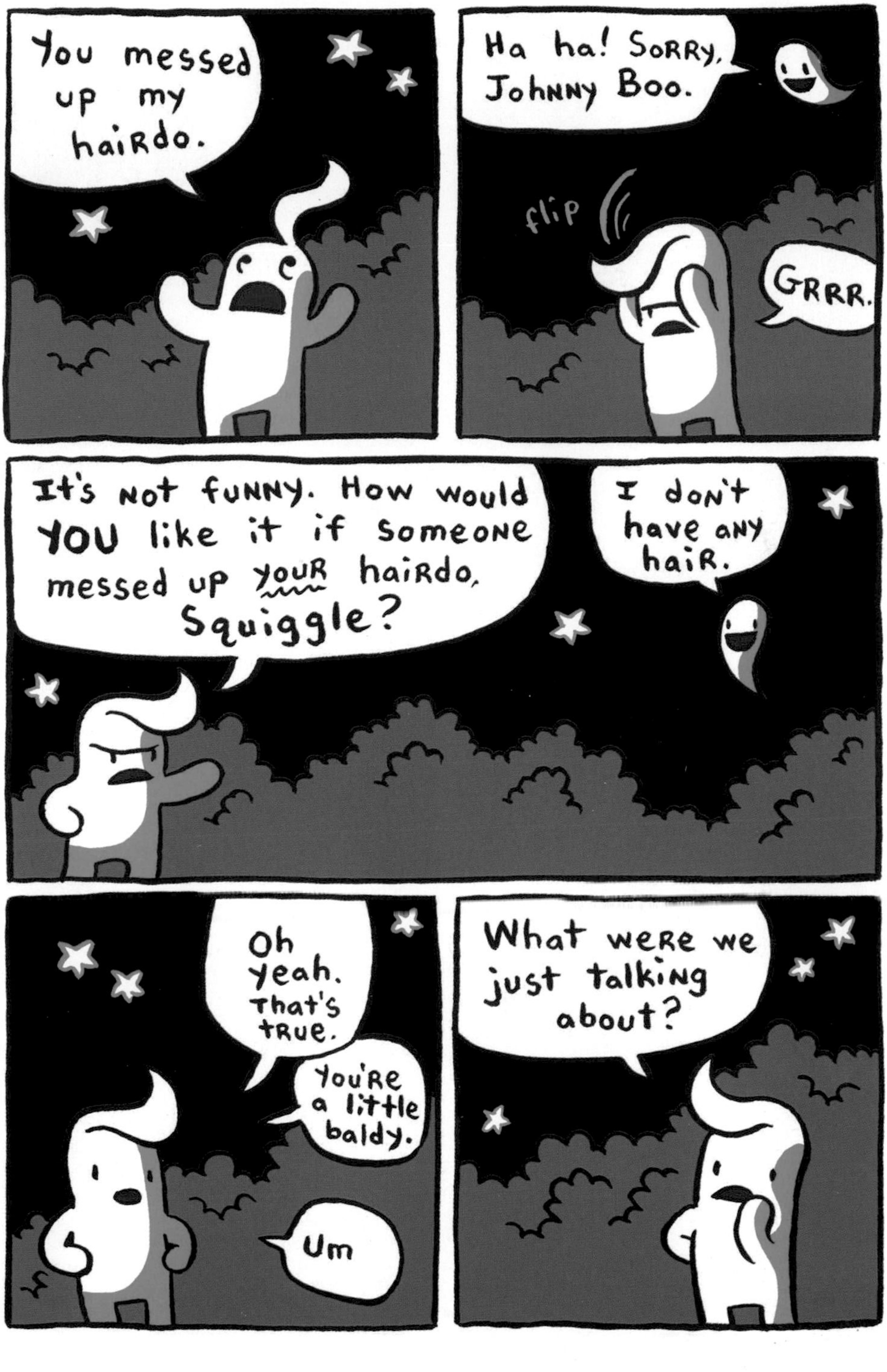
You messed up my hairdo.
Ha ha! SORRY, Johnny Boo.
flip
GRRR.
It's not funny. How would YOU like it if someone messed up YOUR hairdo, Squiggle?
I don't have any hair.
Oh yeah. That's true.
You're a little baldy.
Um
What were we just talking about?

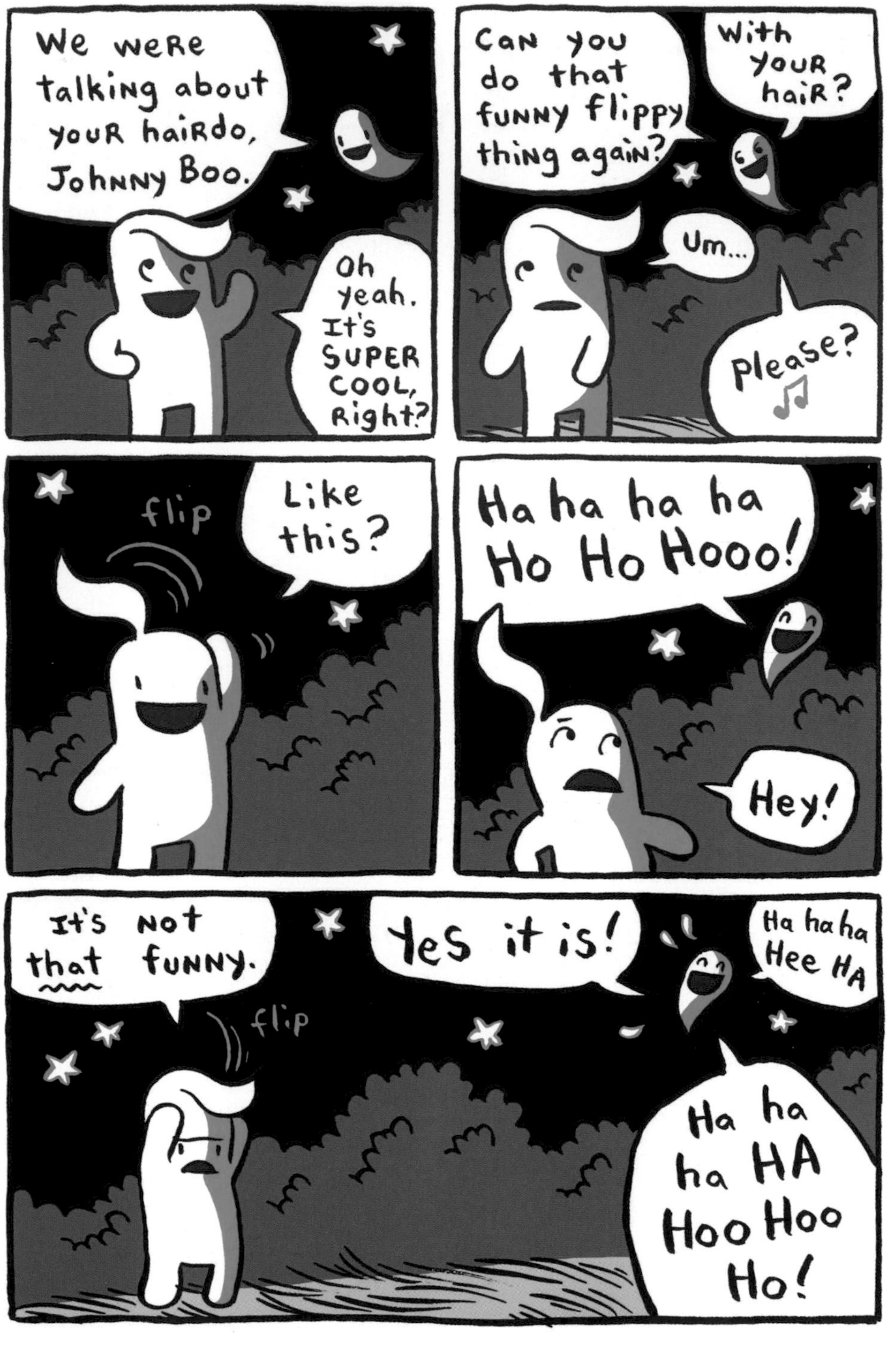
We were talking about your hairdo, Johnny Boo.
Oh yeah. It's SUPER COOL, Right?
Can you do that funny flippy thing again?
With your hair?
Um...
Please?
flip
Like this?
Ha ha ha ha Ho Ho Hooo!
Hey!
It's not that funny.
flip
Yes it is!
Ha ha ha Hee HA
Ha ha ha HA Hoo Hoo Ho!

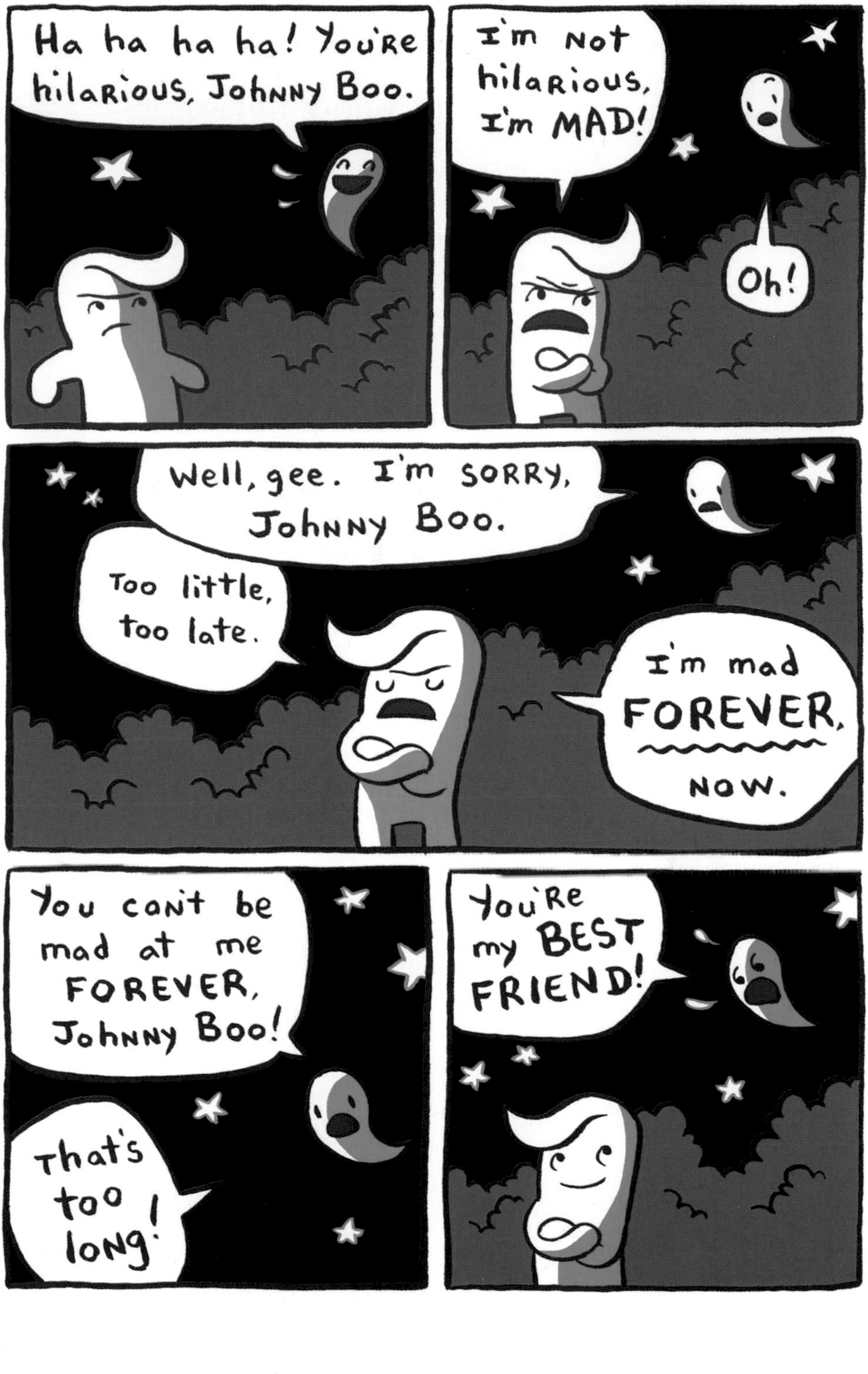
Ha ha ha ha! You're hilarious, Johnny Boo.
I'm not hilarious, I'm MAD!
Oh!
Well, gee. I'm SORRY, Johnny Boo.
Too little, too late.
I'm mad FOREVER, NOW.
You can't be mad at me FOREVER, Johnny Boo!
That's too long!
You're my BEST FRIEND!

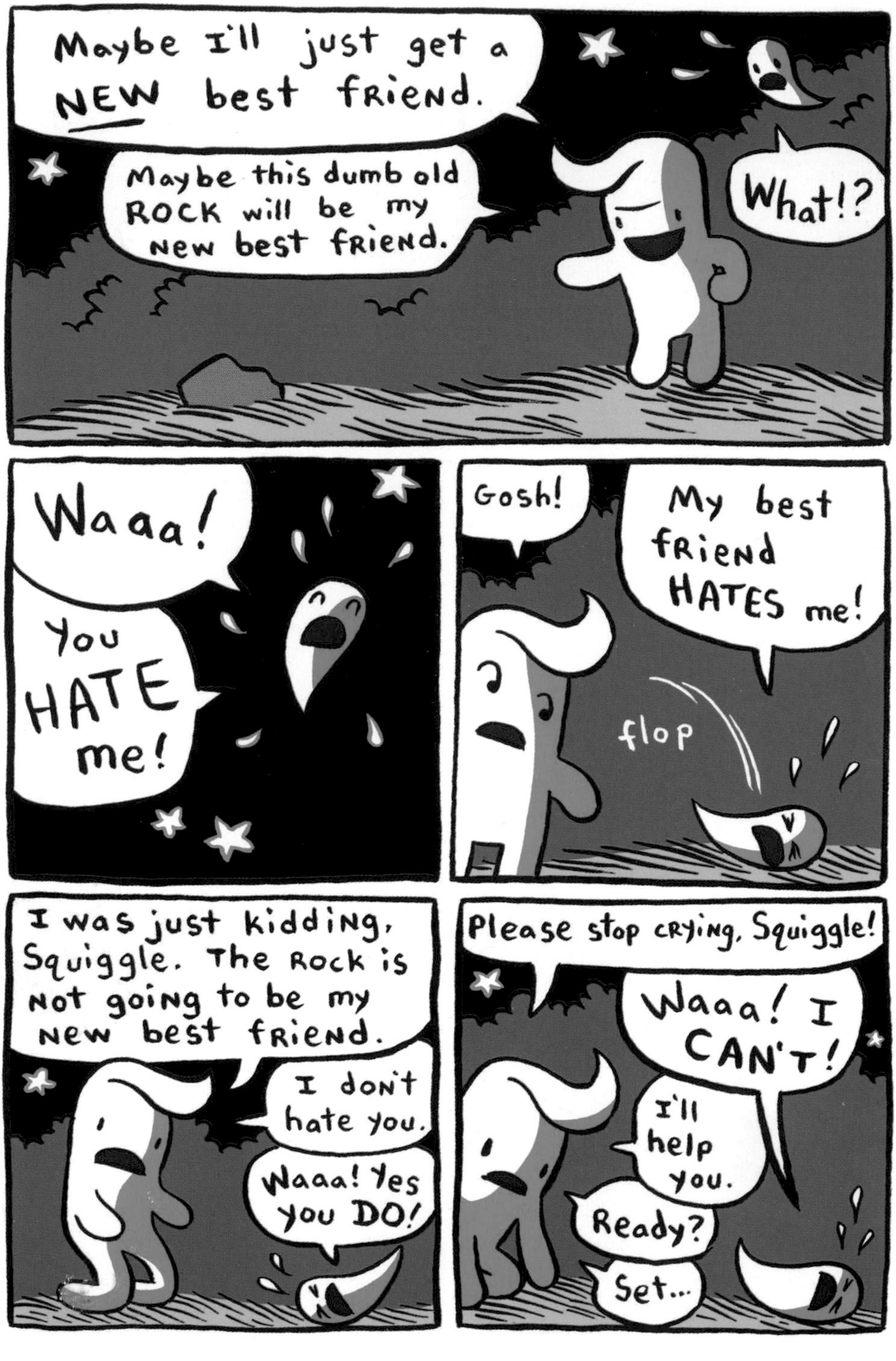

Maybe I'll just get a NEW best friend.
What!?
Maybe this dumb old ROCK will be my new best friend.
Waaa!
You HATE me!
Gosh!
My best friend HATES me!
flop
I was just kidding, Squiggle. The rock is not going to be my new best friend.
I don't hate you.
Waaa! Yes you DO!
Please stop crying, Squiggle!
Waaa! I CAN'T!
I'll help you.
Ready?
Set...

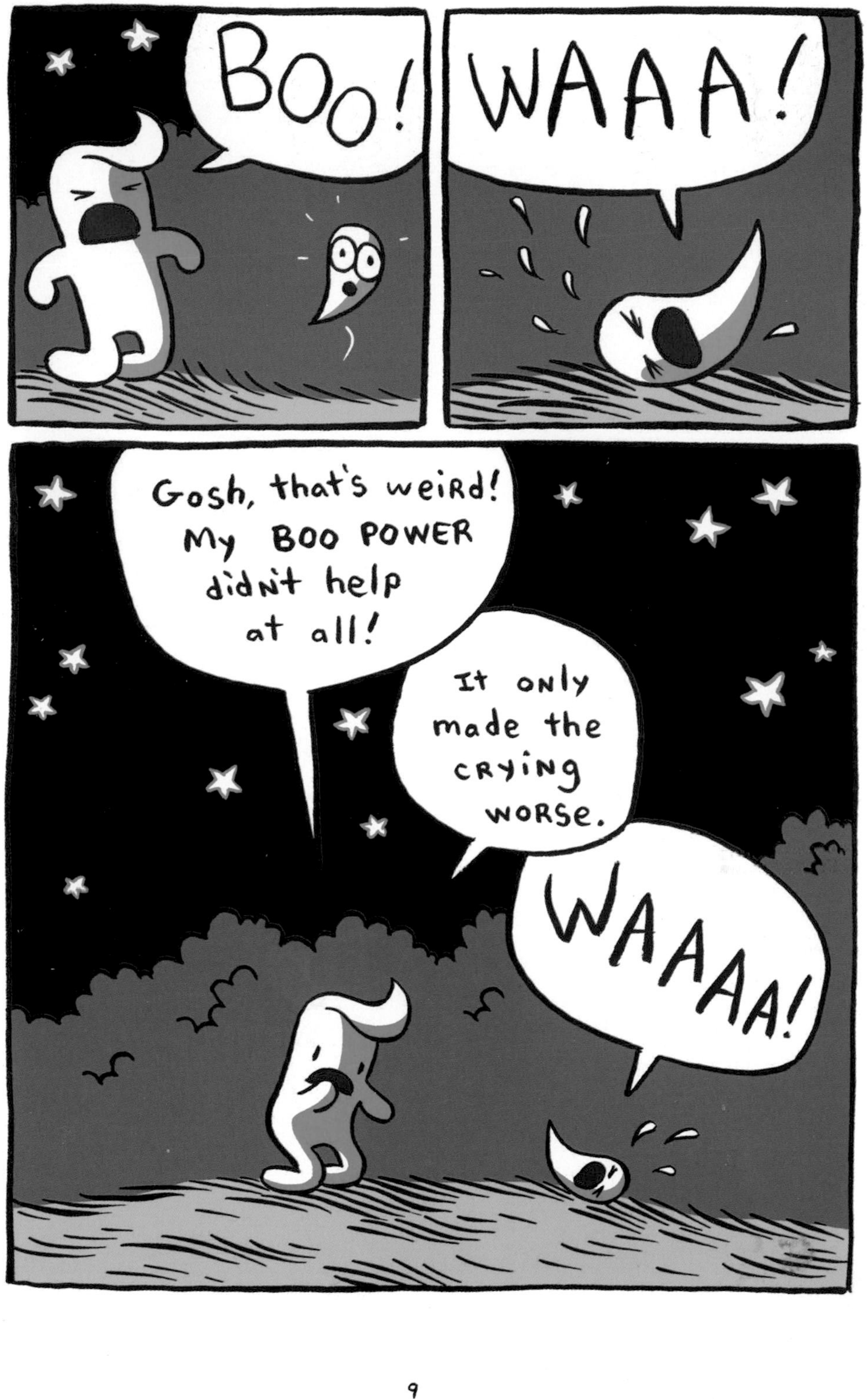
BOO!
WAAA!
Gosh, that's weird! My BOO POWER didn't help at all!
It only made the crying worse.
WAAAAA!

CHAPTER TWO:

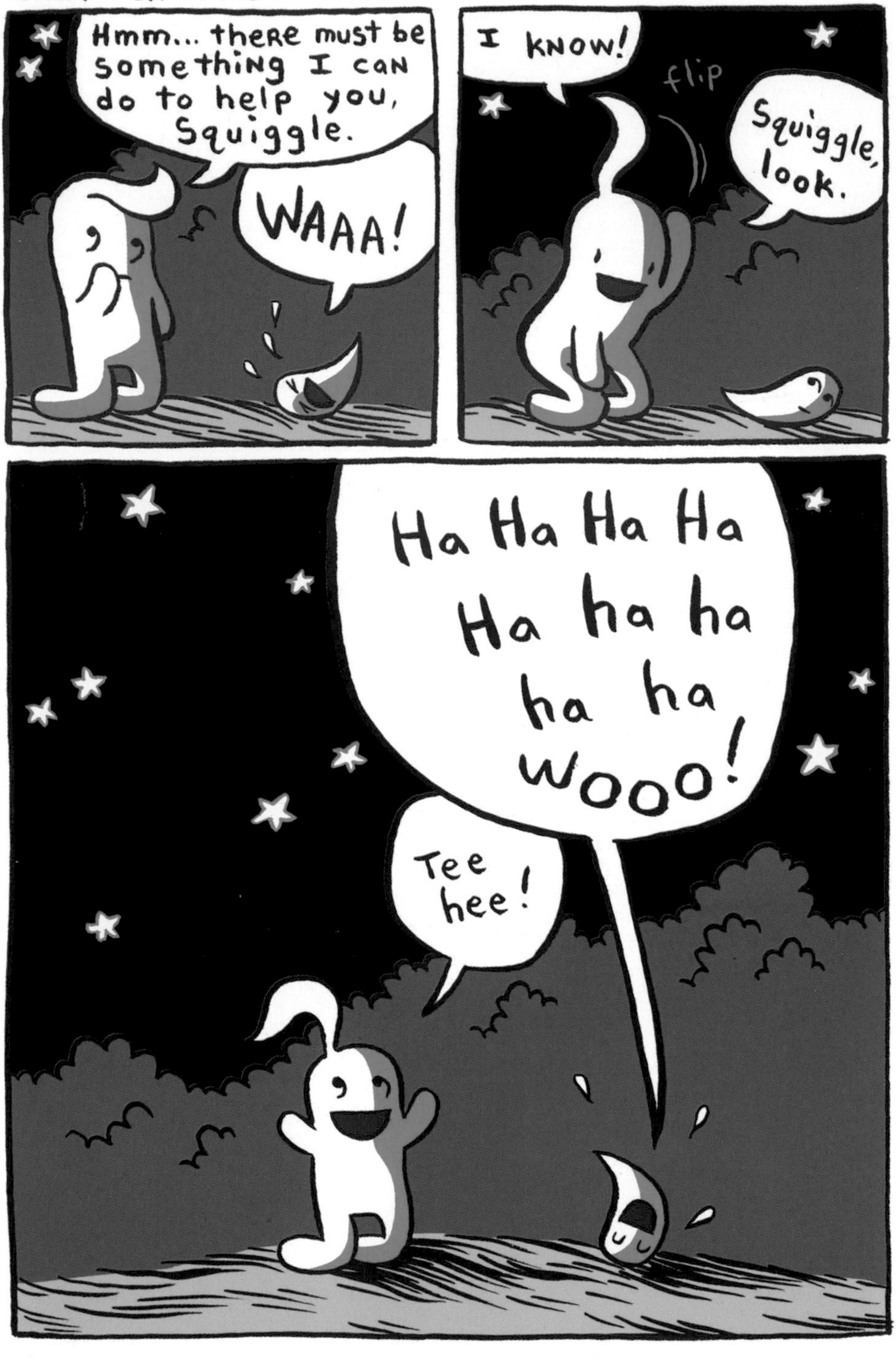
Hmm... there must be something I can do to help you, Squiggle.
WAAA!
I KNOW!
flip
Squiggle, look.
Ha Ha Ha Ha Ha ha ha ha ha WOOO!
Tee hee!

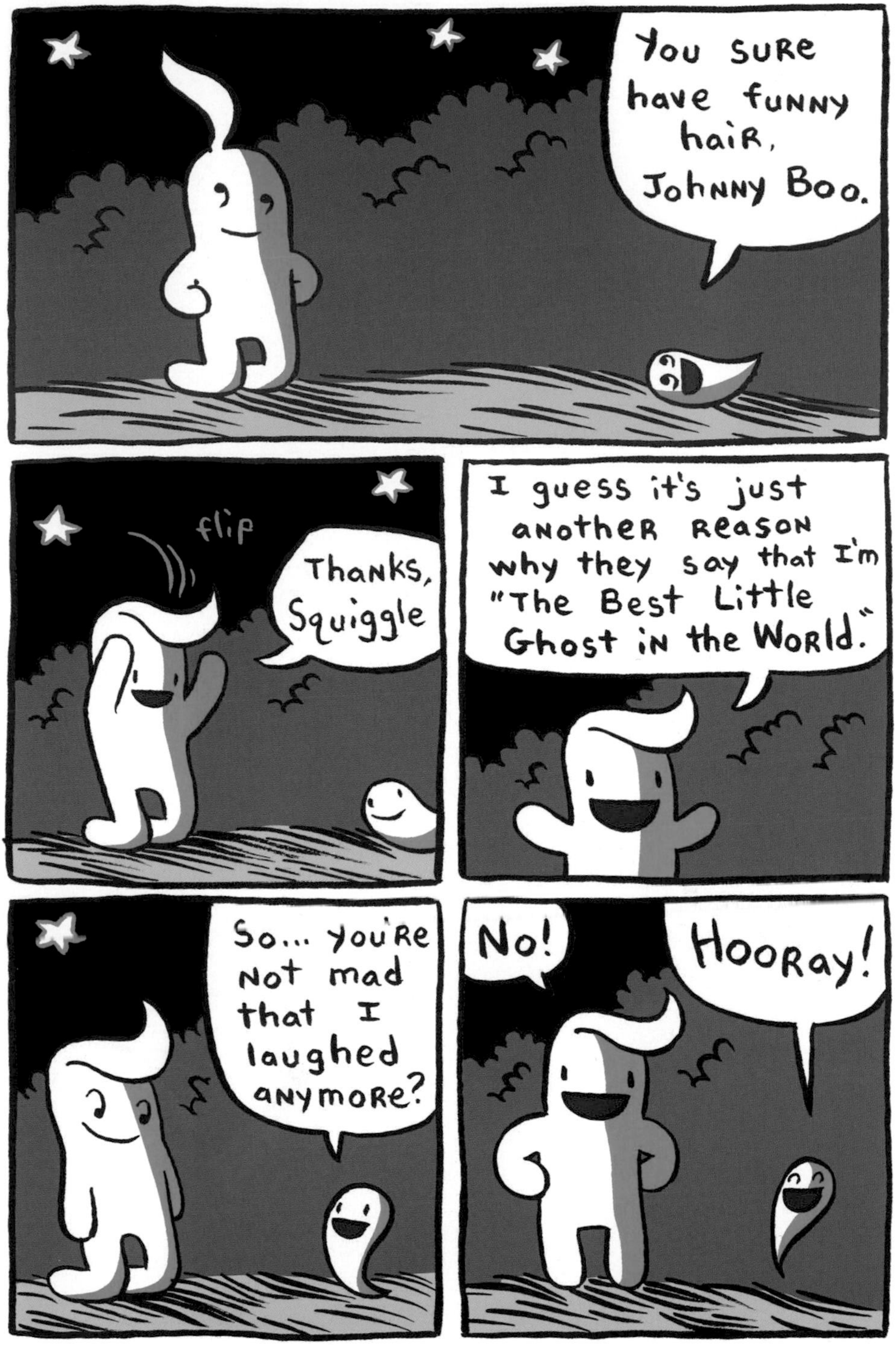
You sure have funny hair, Johnny Boo.
flip
Thanks, Squiggle
I guess it's just another reason why they say that I'm "The Best Little Ghost in the World."
So... you're not mad that I laughed anymore?
No!
Hooray!

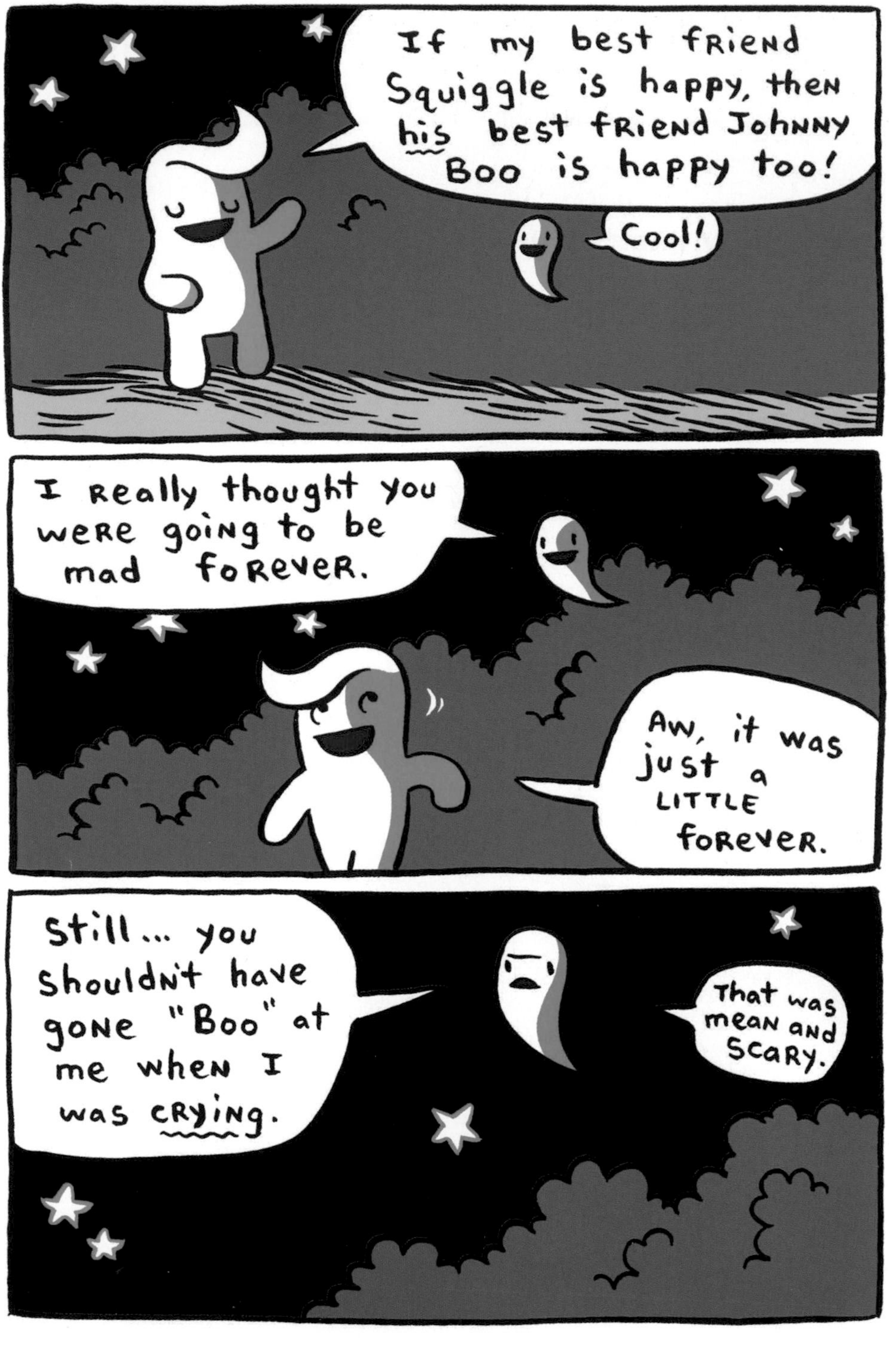
If my best friend Squiggle is happy, then his best friend Johnny Boo is happy too!
Cool!
I really thought you were going to be mad forever.
Aw, it was just a little forever.
Still... you shouldn't have gone "Boo" at me when I was crying.
That was mean and scary.

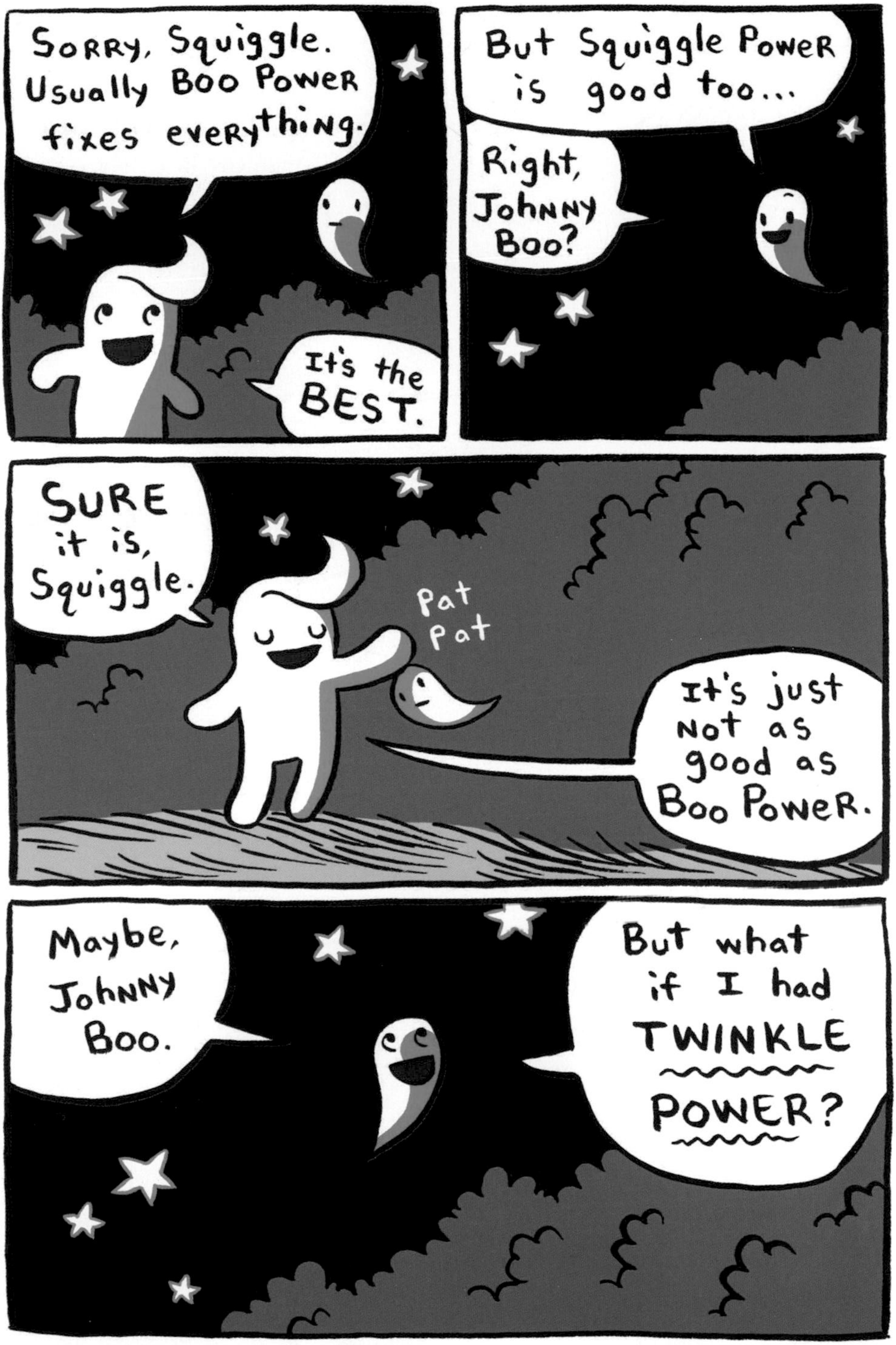
Sorry, Squiggle. Usually Boo Power fixes everything.
It's the BEST.
But Squiggle Power is good too...
Right, Johnny Boo?
SURE it is, Squiggle.
Pat pat
It's just not as good as Boo Power.
Maybe, Johnny Boo.
But what if I had TWINKLE POWER?

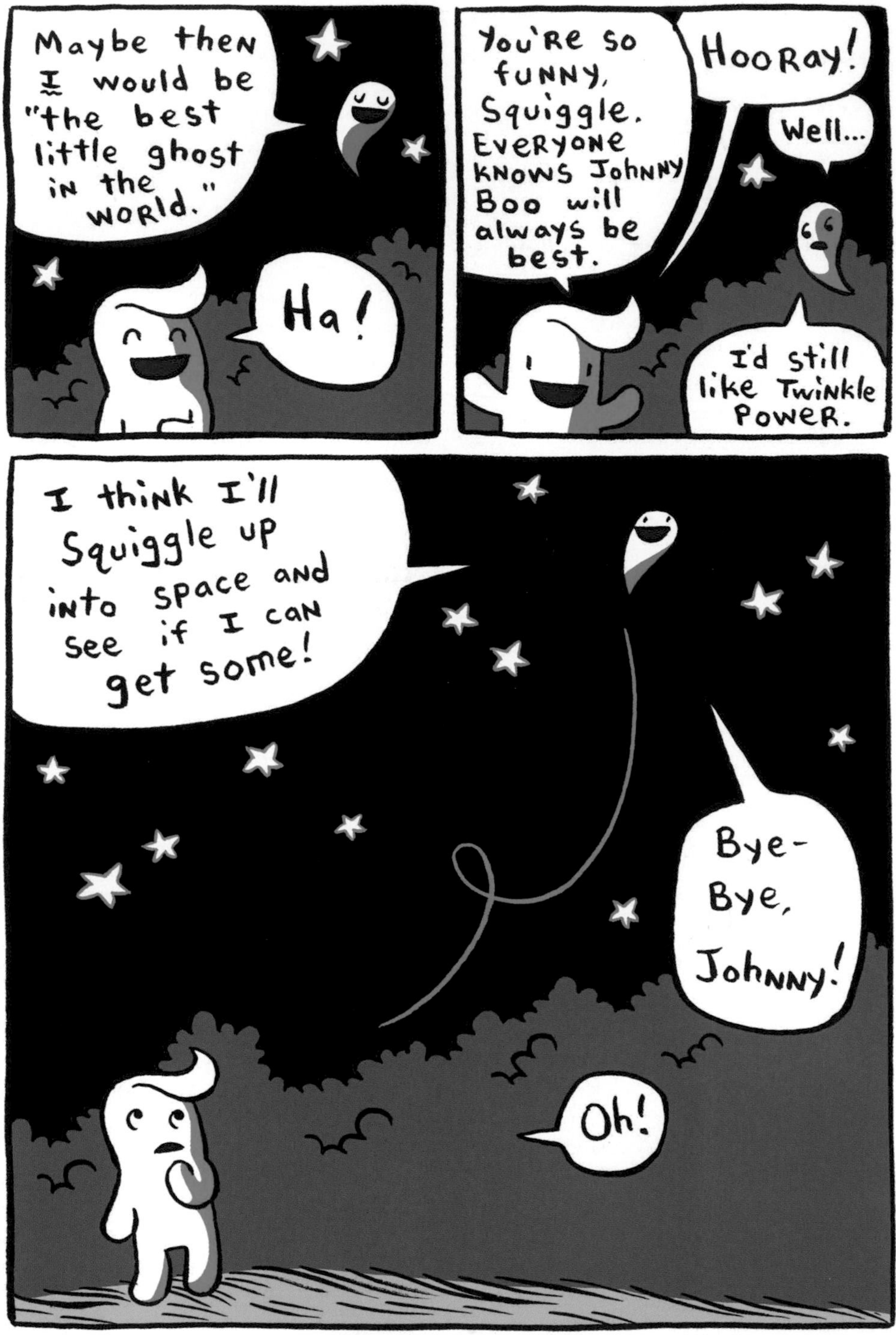
Maybe then I would be "the best little ghost in the world."
Ha!
You're so funny, Squiggle. Everyone knows Johnny Boo will always be best.
Hooray!
Well...
I'd still like Twinkle Power.
I think I'll Squiggle up into space and see if I can get some!
Bye-Bye, Johnny!
Oh!

CHAPTER THREE:

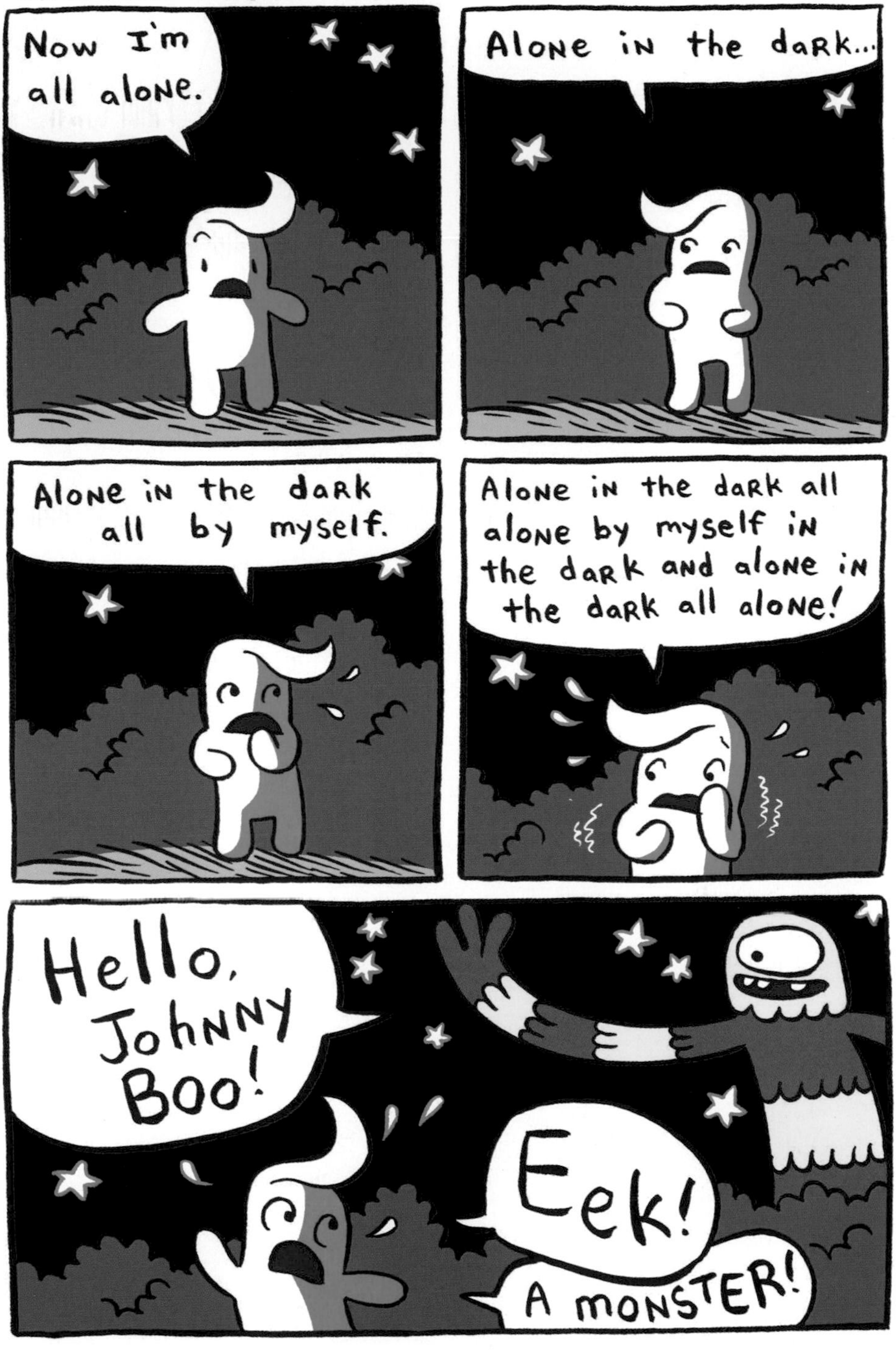
Now I'm all alone.
Alone in the dark...
Alone in the dark all by myself.
Alone in the dark all alone by myself in the dark and alone in the dark all alone!
Hello, Johnny Boo!
Eek!
A MONSTER!

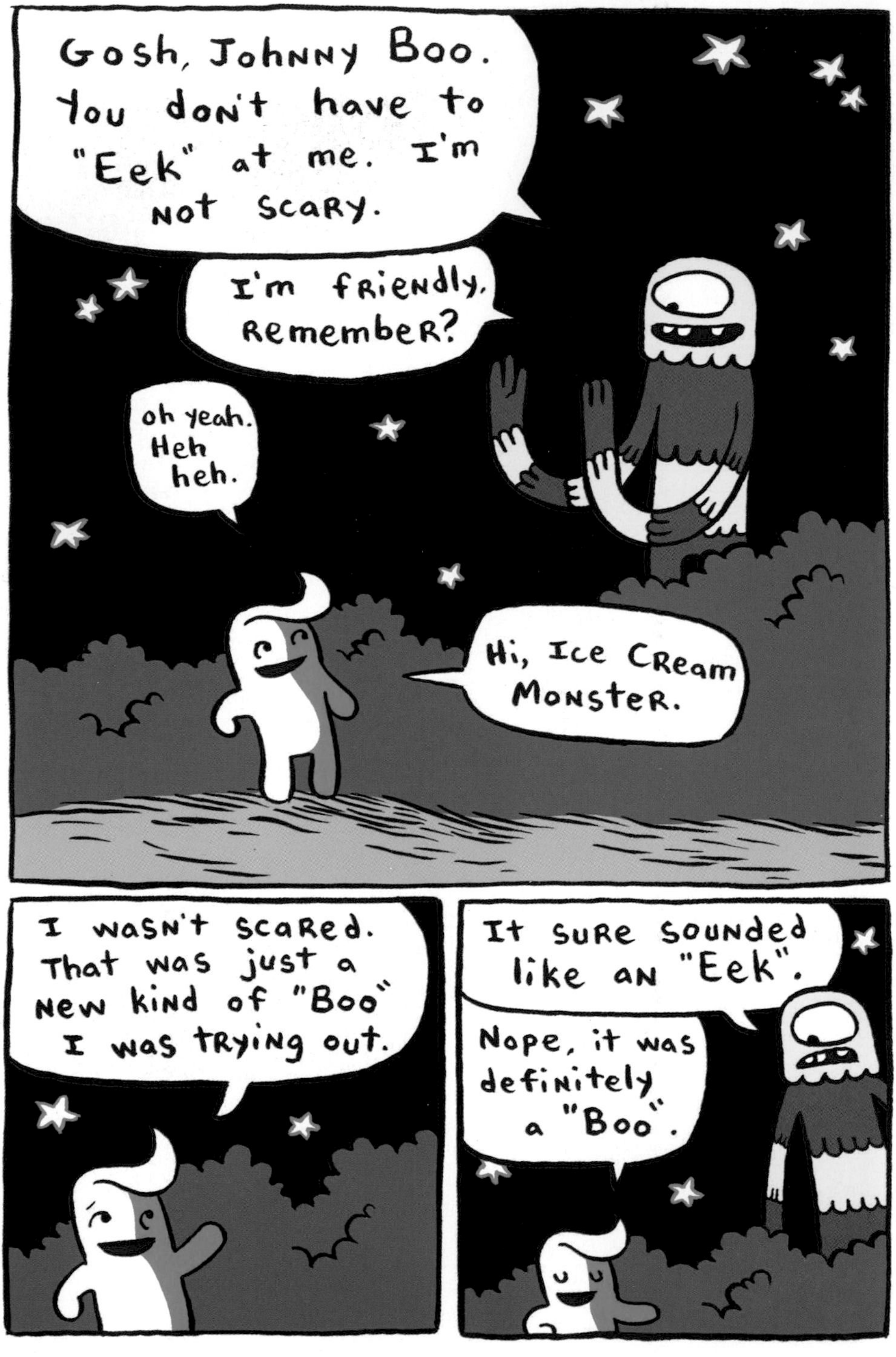
Gosh, Johnny Boo. You don't have to "Eek" at me. I'm not scary.
I'm friendly, remember?
oh yeah. Heh heh.
Hi, Ice Cream Monster.
I wasn't scared. That was just a new kind of "Boo" I was trying out.
It sure sounded like an "Eek".
Nope, it was definitely a "Boo".

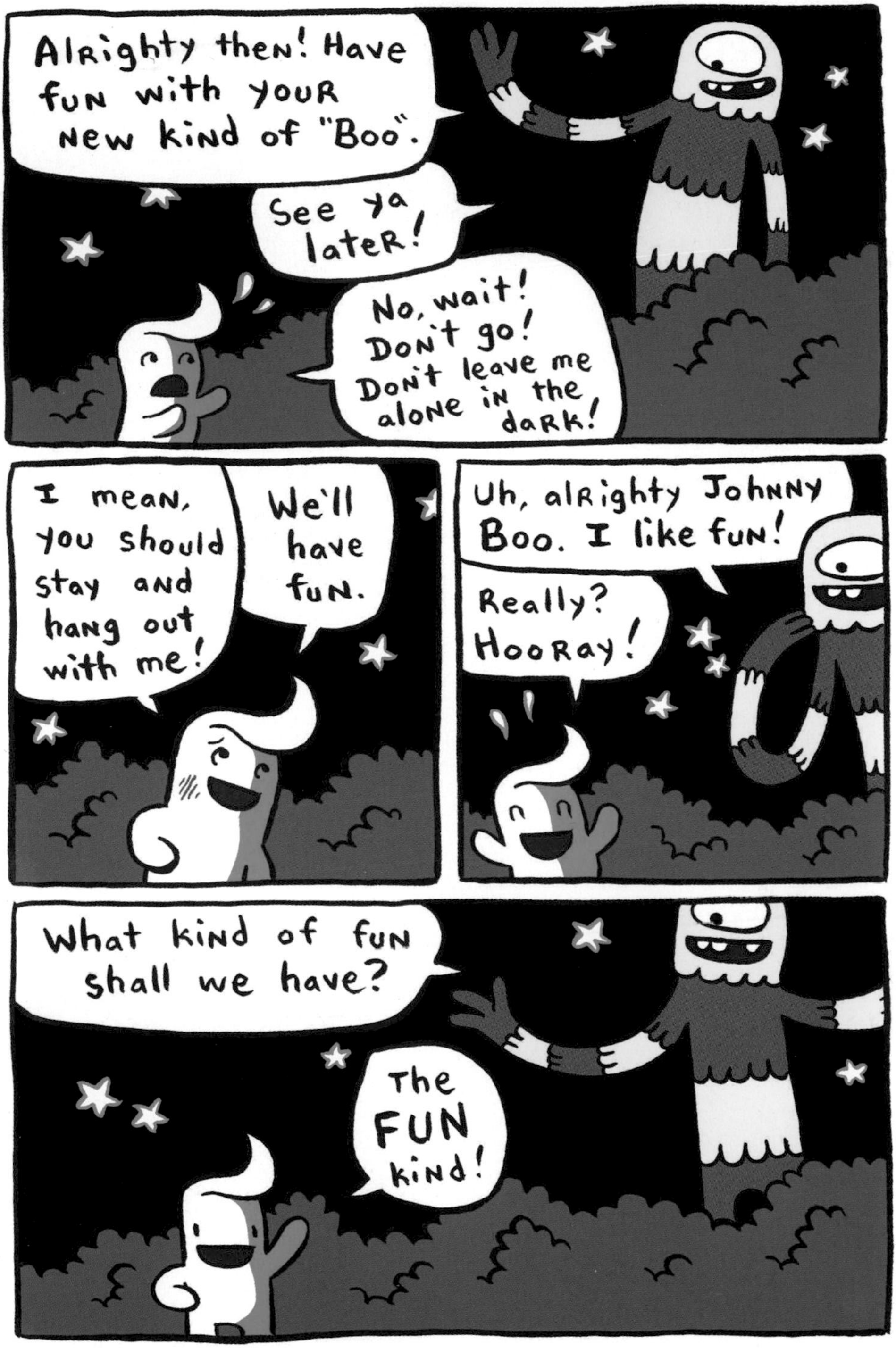
Alrighty then! Have fun with your new kind of "Boo".
See ya later!
No, wait! Don't go! Don't leave me alone in the dark!
I mean, you should stay and hang out with me!
We'll have fun.
Uh, alrighty Johnny Boo. I like fun!
Really? Hooray!
What kind of fun shall we have?
The FUN kind!

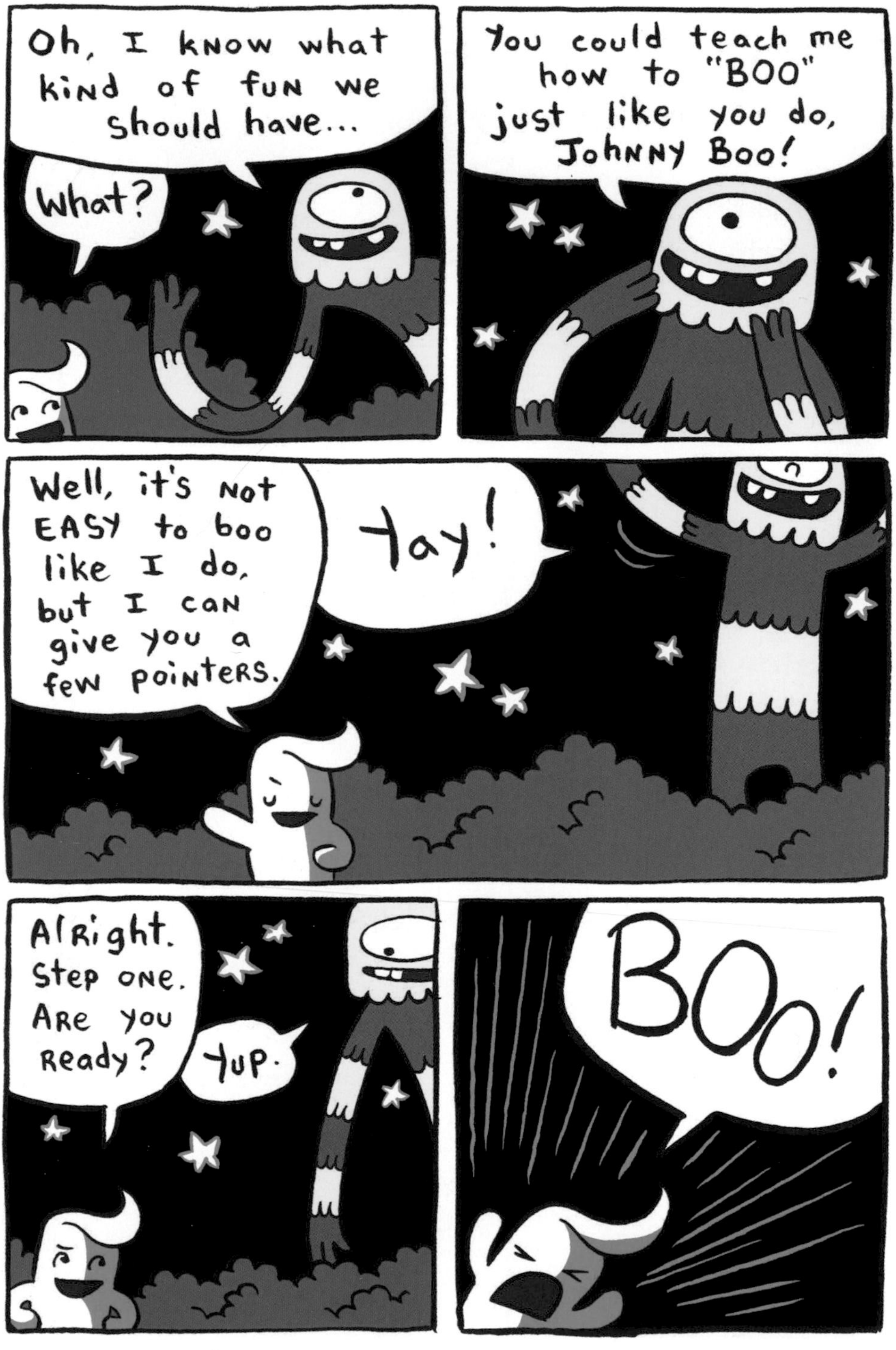
Oh, I know what kind of fun we should have...
What?
You could teach me how to "BOO" just like you do, Johnny Boo!
Well, it's not EASY to boo like I do, but I can give you a few pointers.
Yay!
Alright. Step one. Are you ready?
Yup.
BOO!

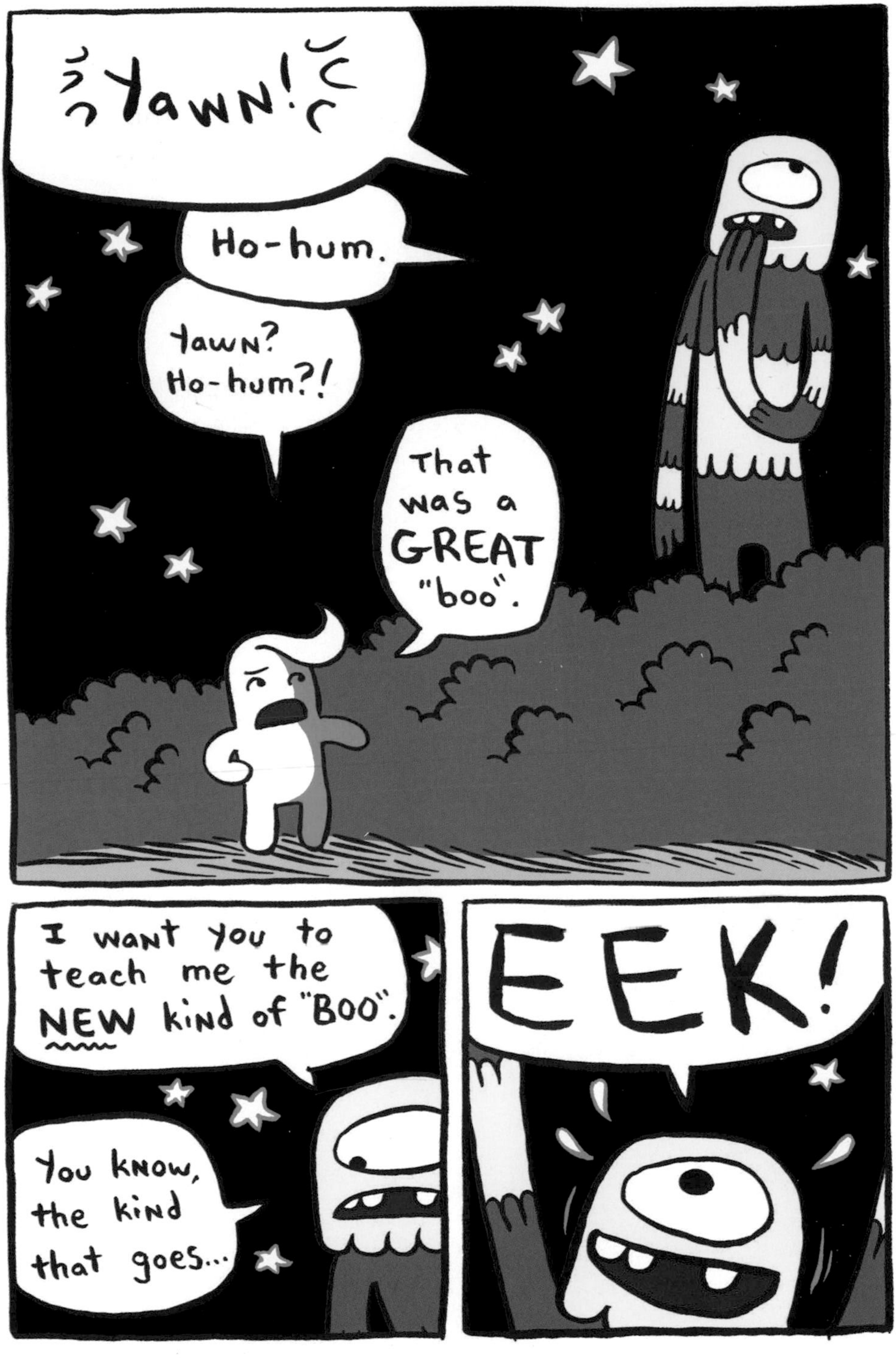
YAWN!
Ho-hum.
Yawn? Ho-hum?!
That was a GREAT "boo".
I want you to teach me the NEW kind of "BOO".
You know, the kind that goes...
EEK!

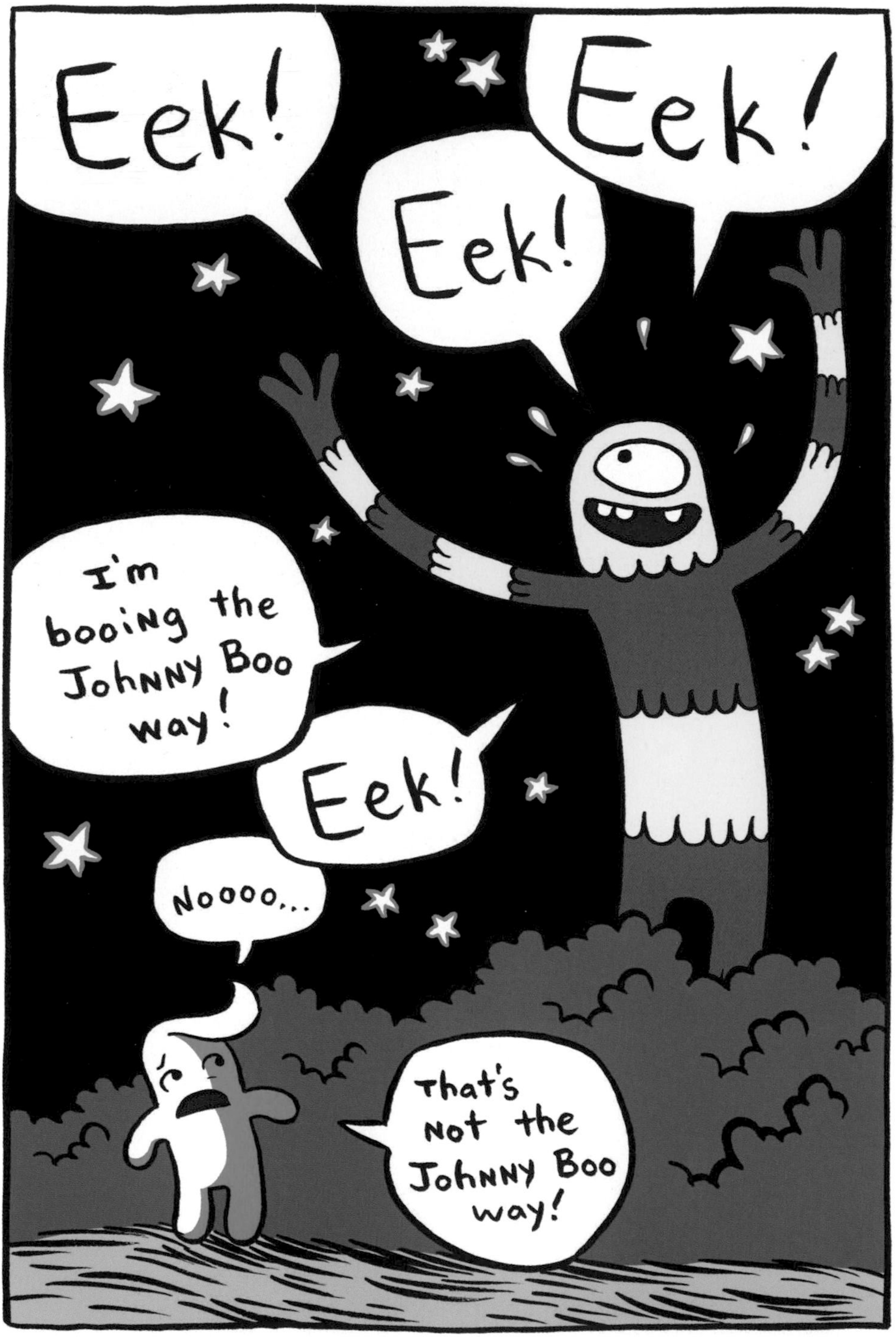
Eek!
Eek!
Eek!
I'm booing the Johnny Boo way!
Eek!
Noooo...
That's not the Johnny Boo way!

CHAPTER FOUR:

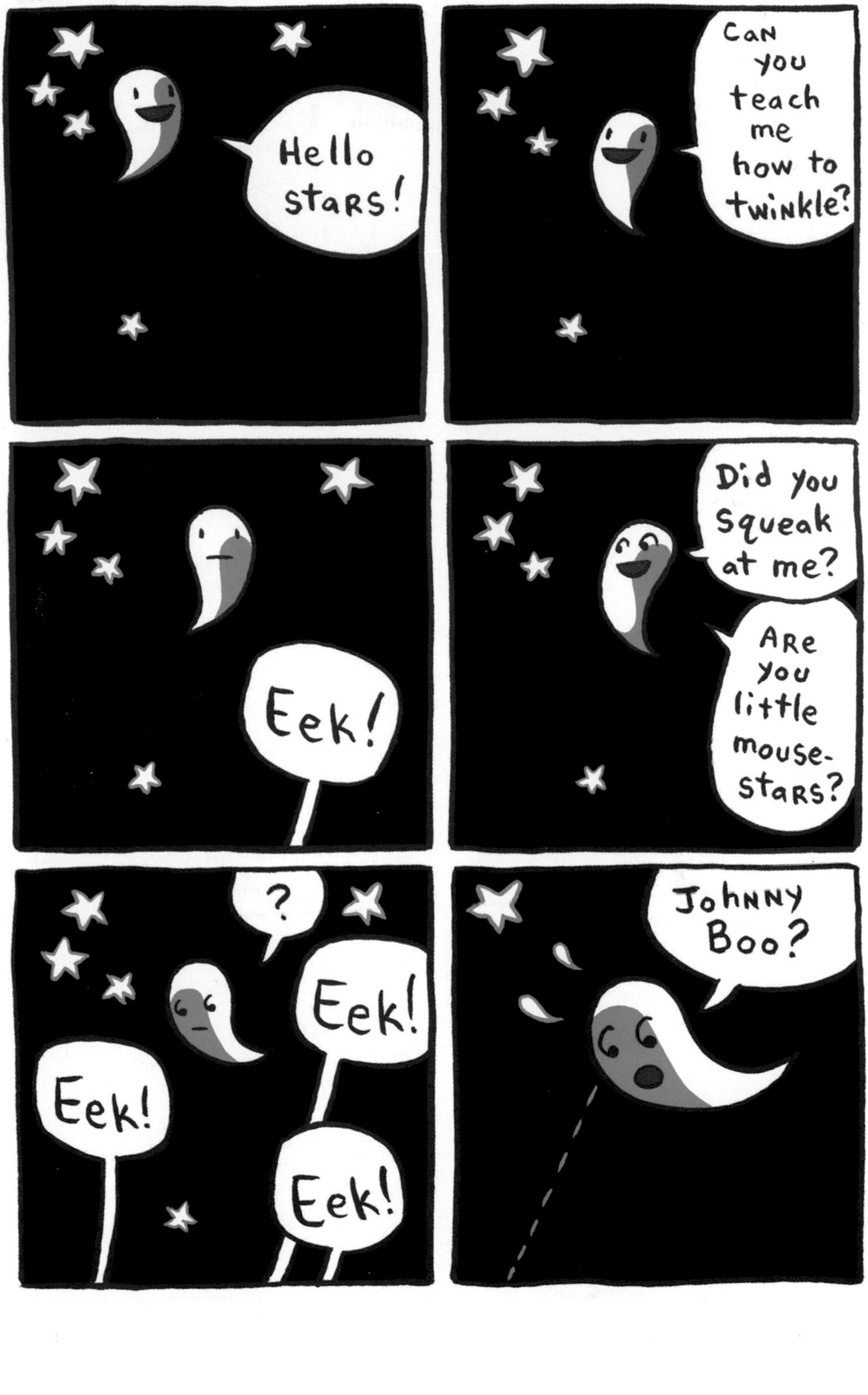
Hello STARS!
Can you teach me how to twinkle?
Eek!
Did you squeak at me?
ARe you little mouse-stars?
?
Eek!
Eek!
Eek!
JohNNY Boo?

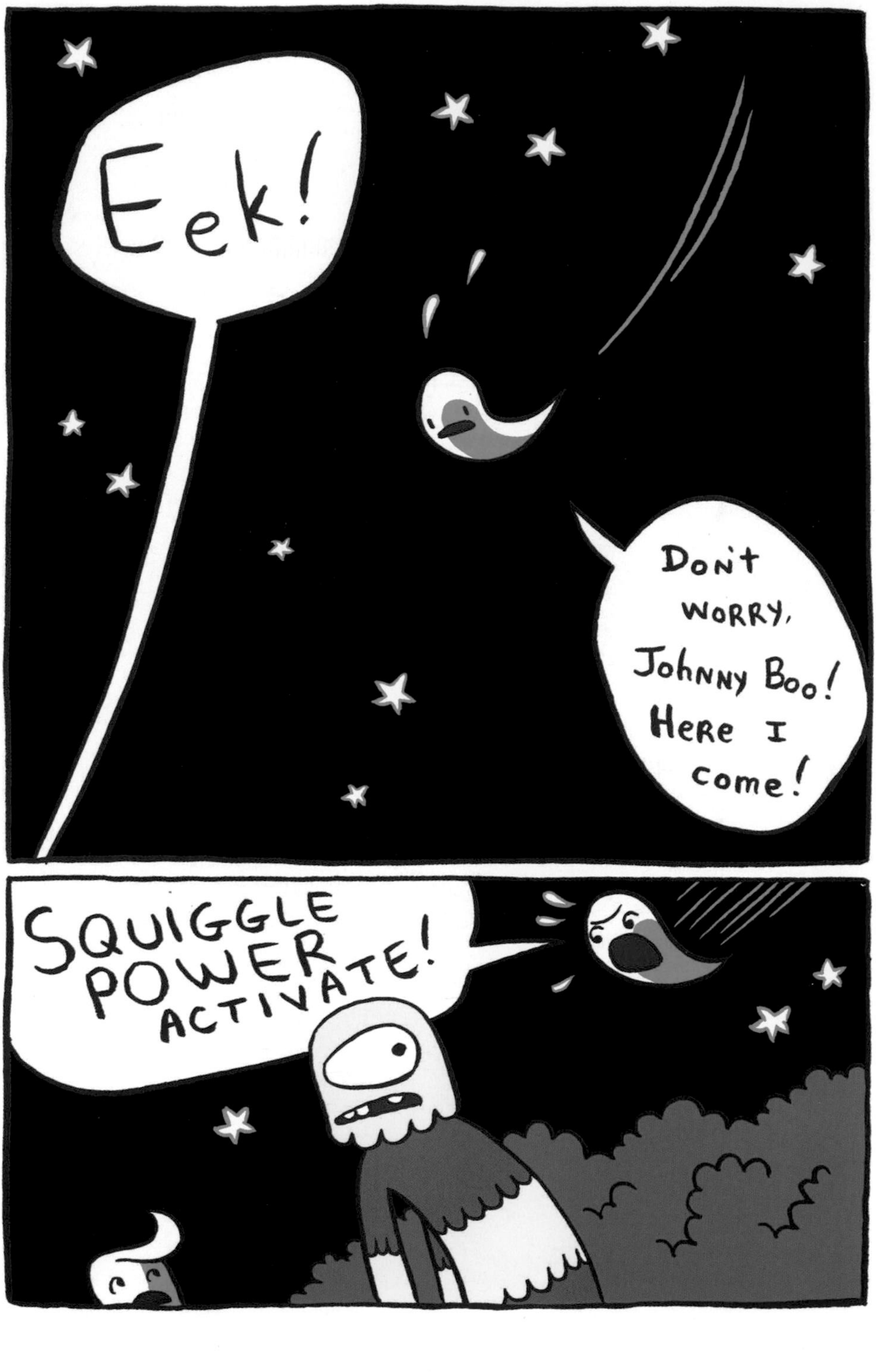
Eek!
Don't worry, Johnny Boo! Here I come!
SQUIGGLE POWER ACTIVATE!

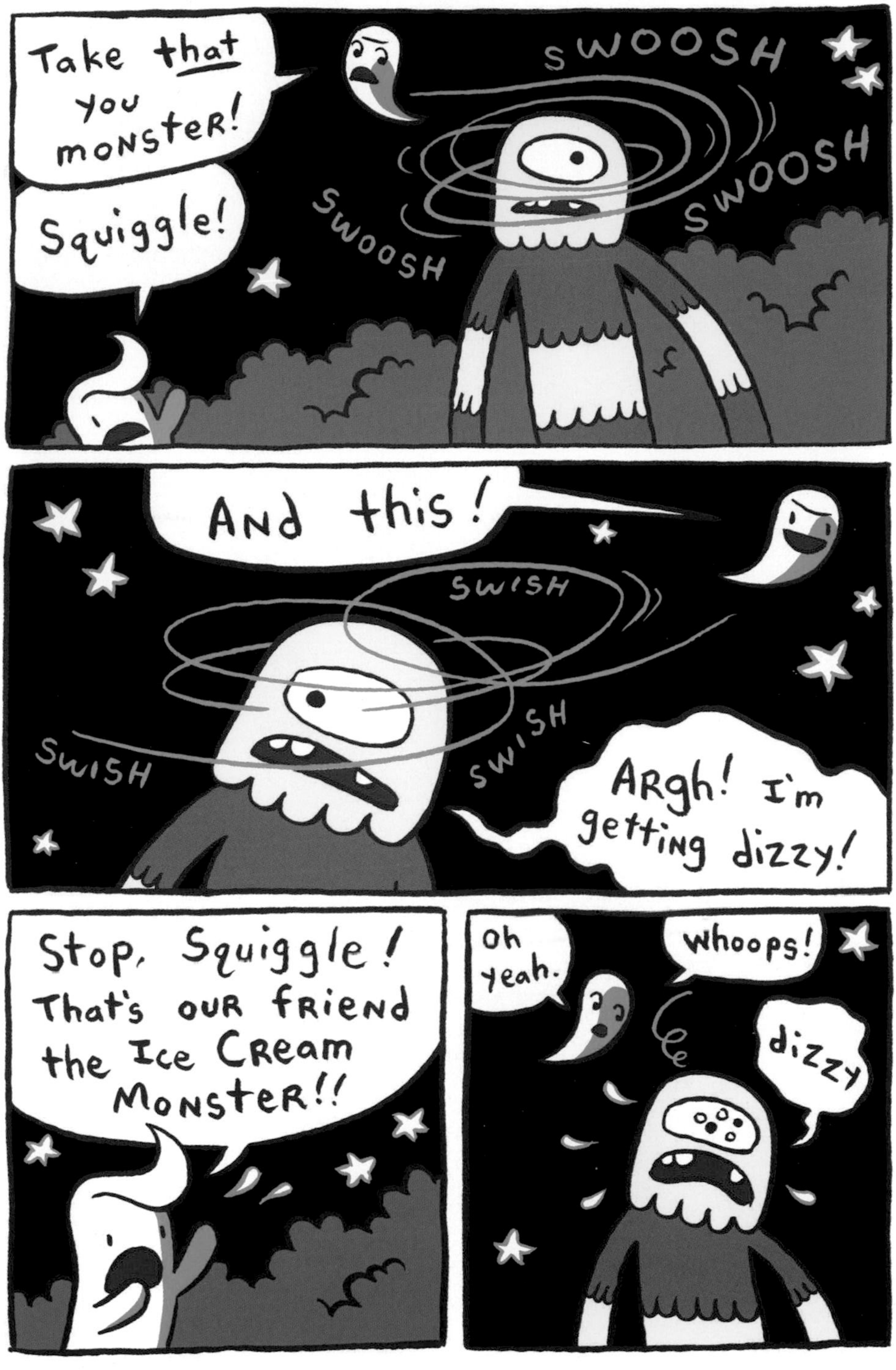
Take that you monster!
Squiggle!
SWOOSH
SWOOSH
SWOOSH
And this!
SWISH
SWISH
SWISH
Argh! I'm getting dizzy!
Stop, Squiggle! That's our friend the Ice Cream Monster!!
Oh yeah.
Whoops!
dizzy

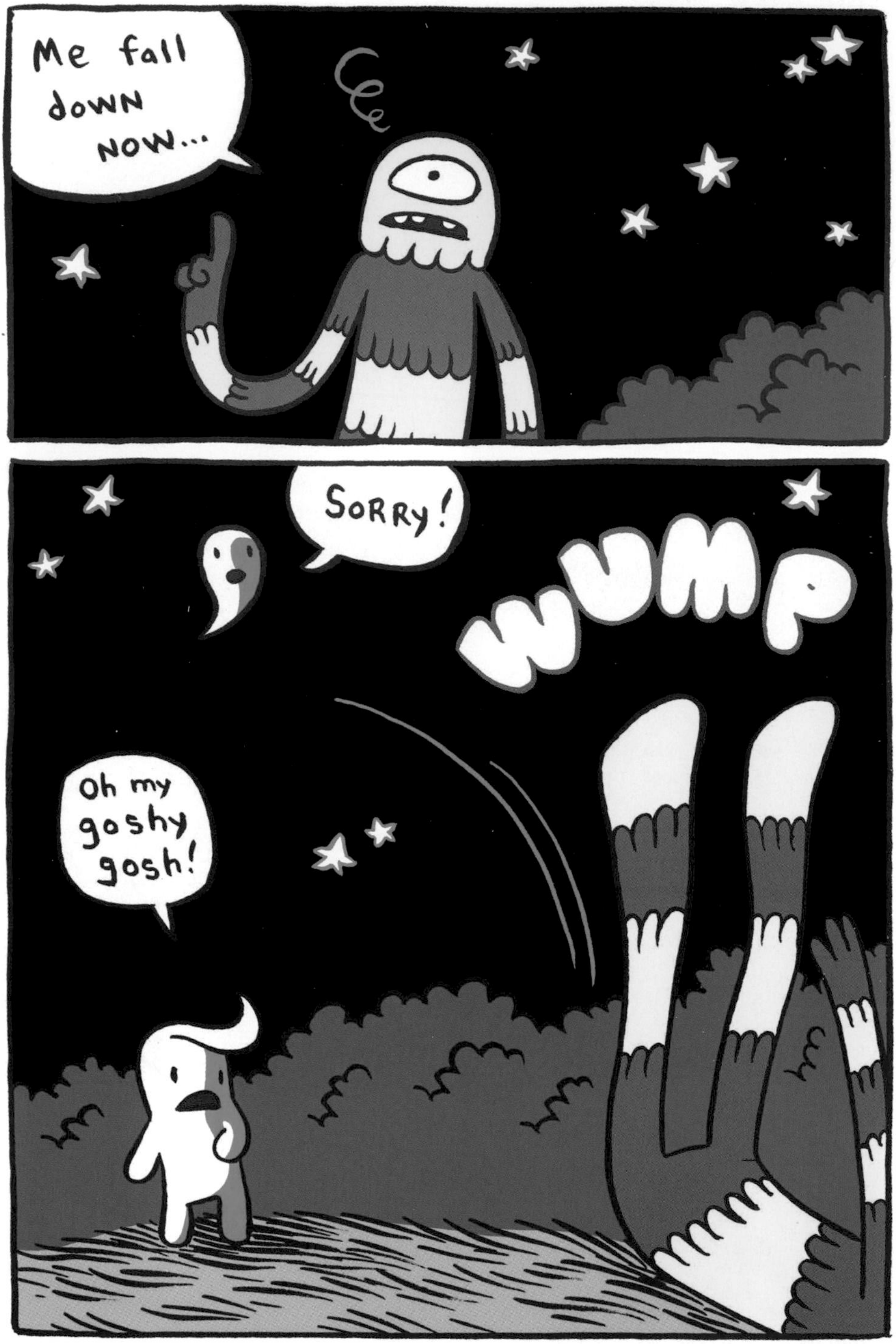
Me fall down now...
Sorry!
WUMP
Oh my goshy gosh!

CHAPTER FIVE:

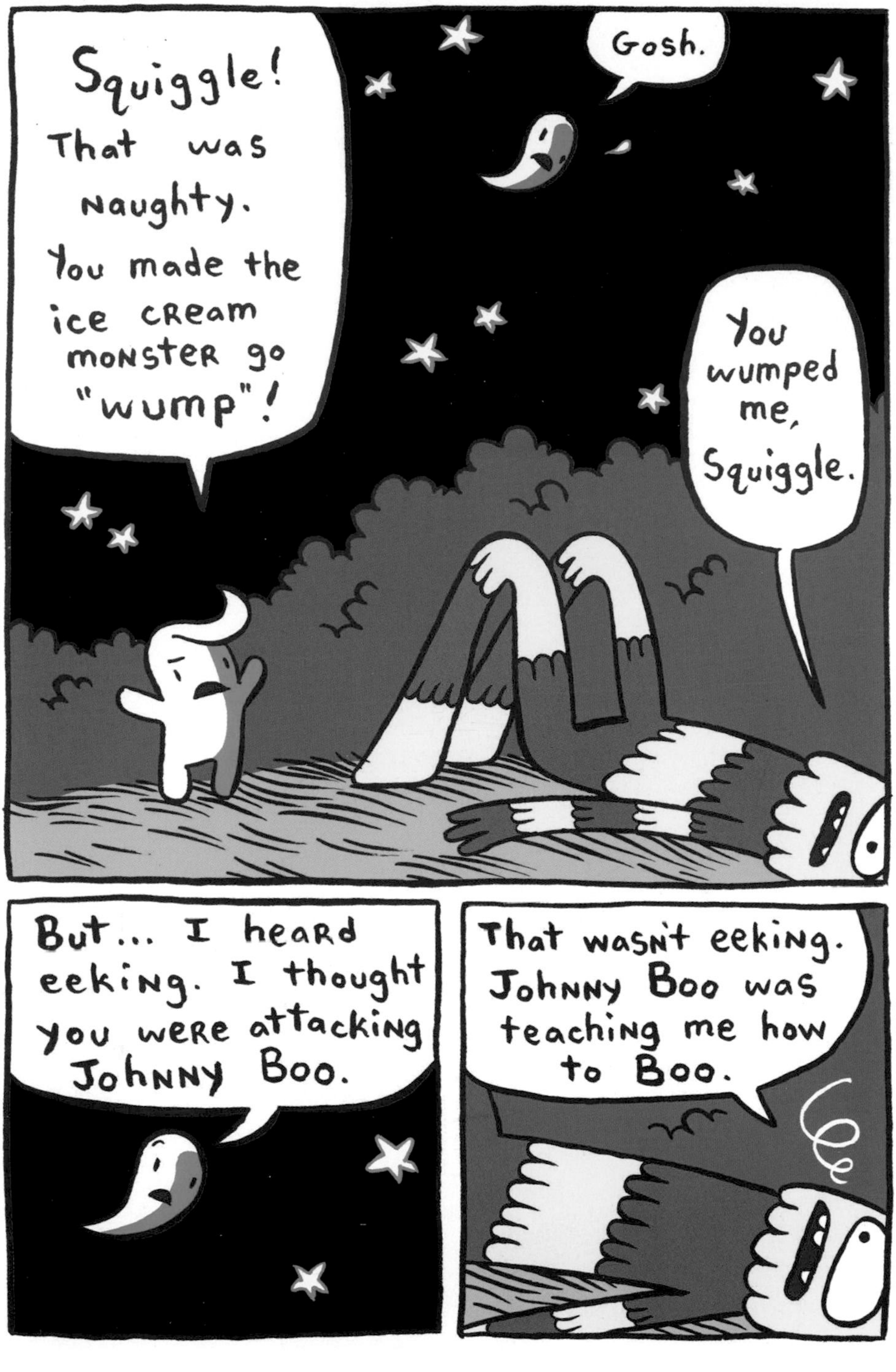
Squiggle! That was naughty. You made the ice cream monster go "wump"!
Gosh.
You wumped me, Squiggle.
But... I heard eeking. I thought you were attacking Johnny Boo.
That wasn't eeking. Johnny Boo was teaching me how to Boo.

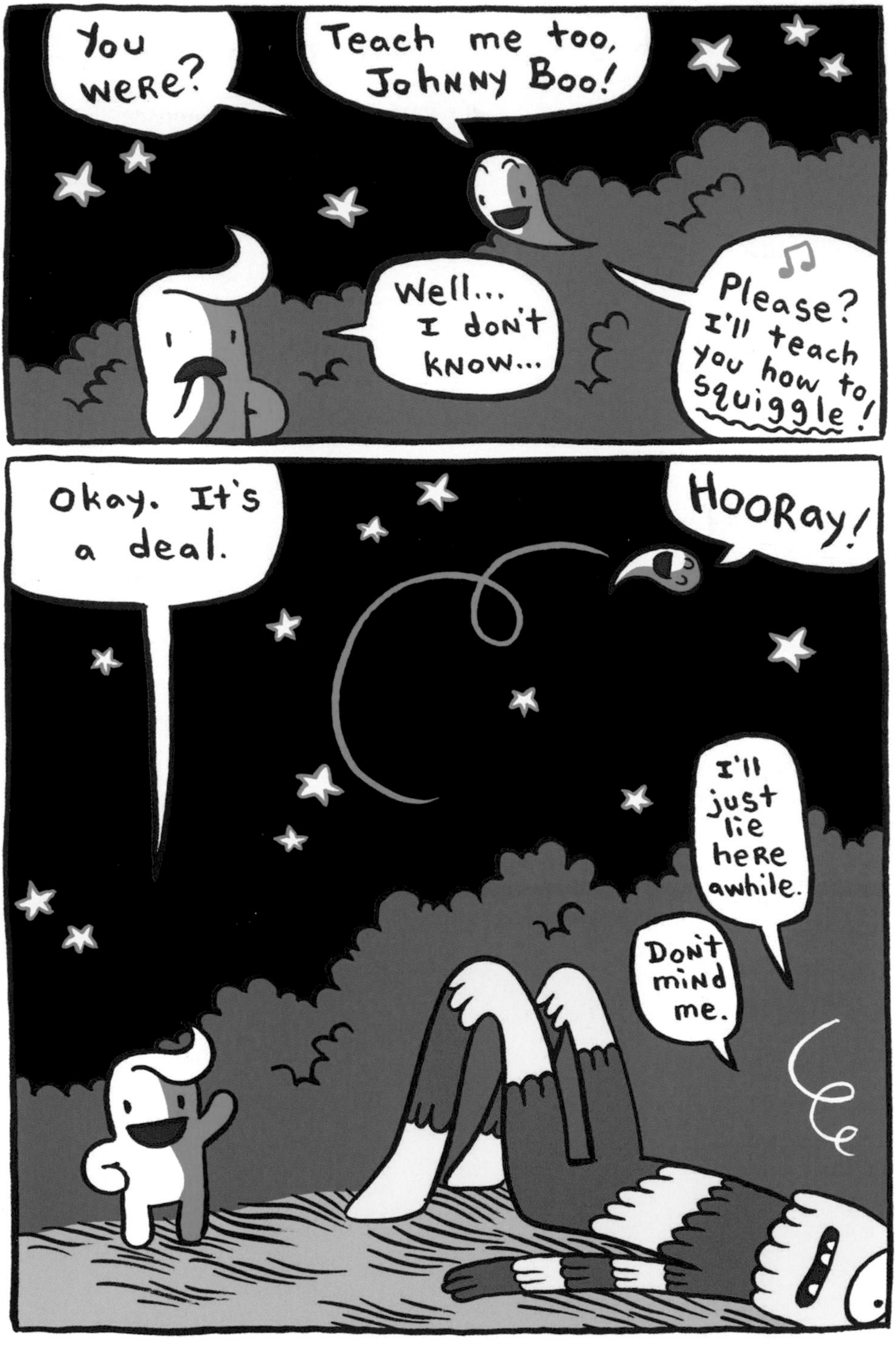
You were?
Teach me too, Johnny Boo!
Well... I don't know...
Please? I'll teach you how to squiggle!
Okay. It's a deal.
HOORAY!
I'll just lie here awhile.
Don't mind me.

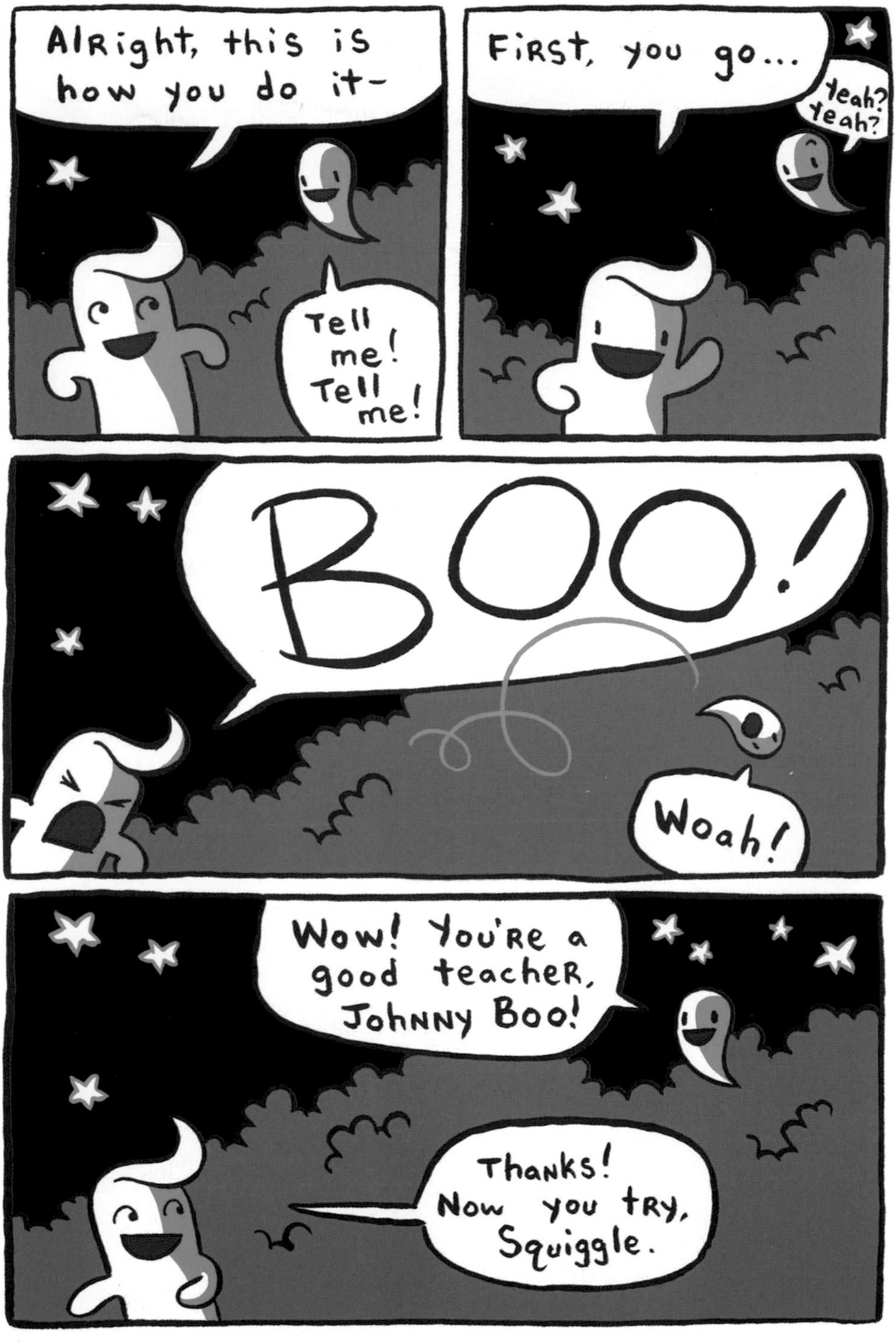
Alright, this is how you do it-
Tell me! Tell me!
First, you go...
Yeah? Yeah?
BOO!
Woah!
Wow! You're a good teacher, Johnny Boo!
Thanks! Now you try, Squiggle.

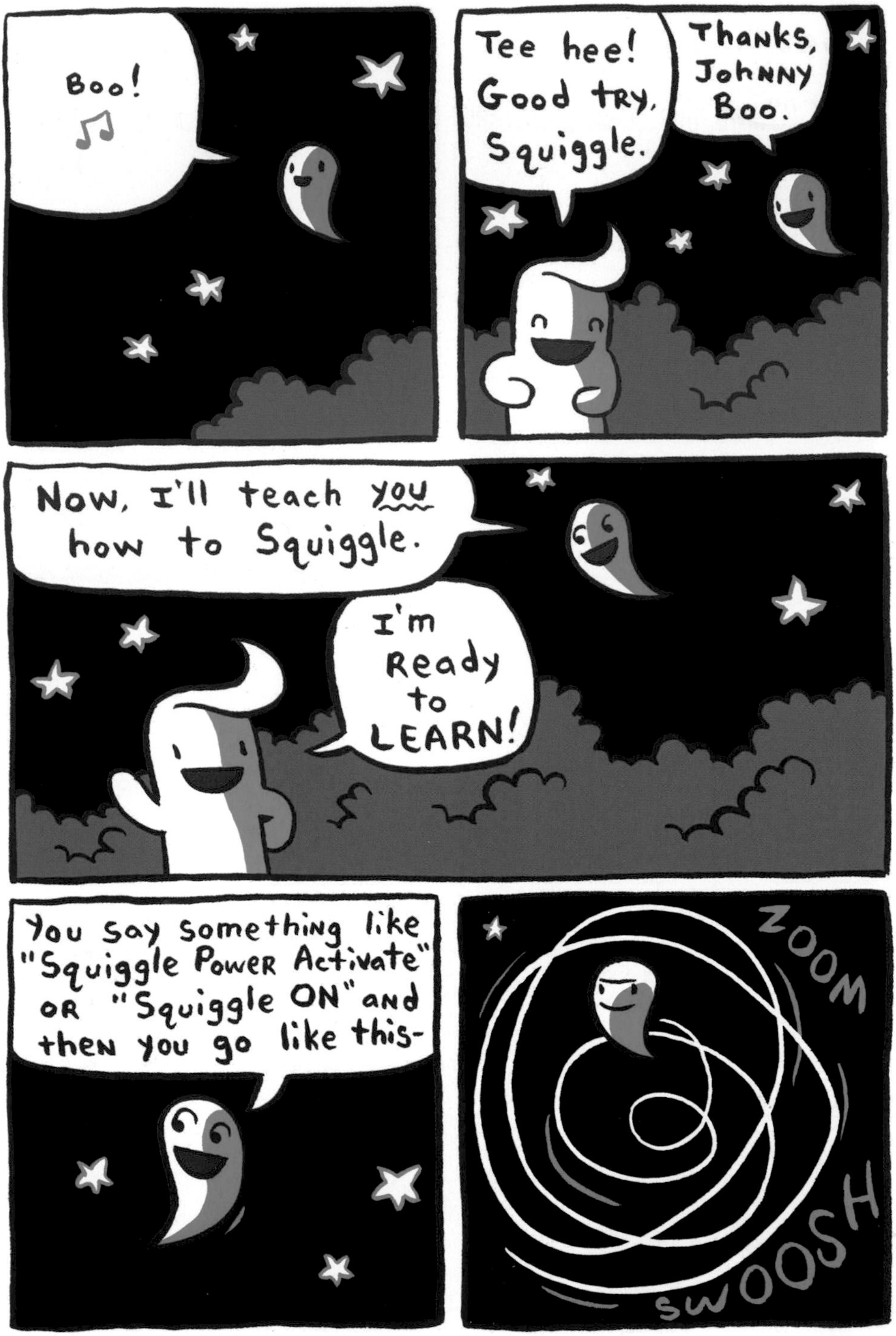
Boo!
Tee hee! Good try, Squiggle.
Thanks, Johnny Boo.
Now, I'll teach you how to Squiggle.
I'm Ready to LEARN!
You say something like "Squiggle Power Activate" or "Squiggle ON" and then you go like this-
ZOOM
SWOOSH

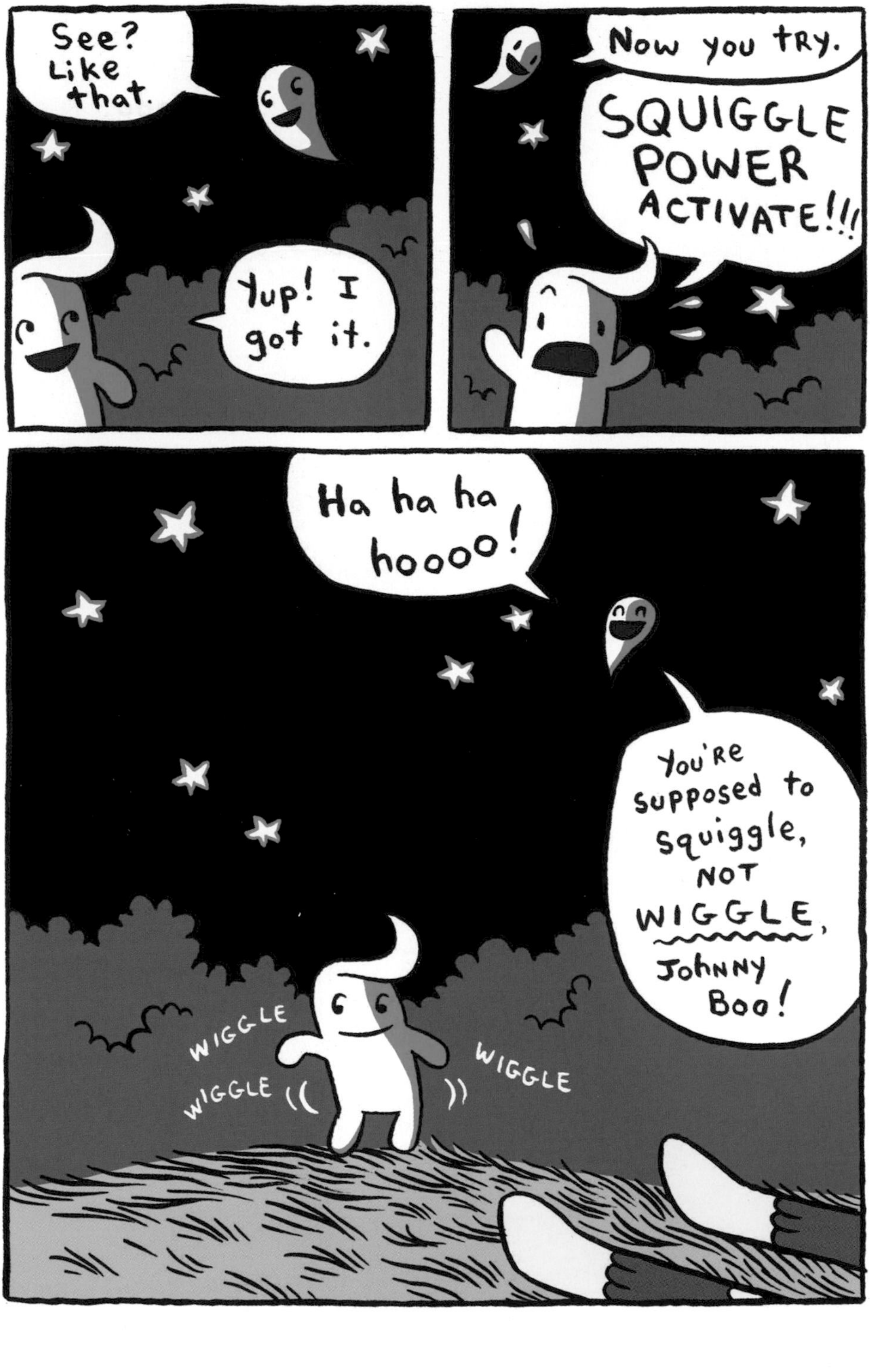
See? Like that.
Yup! I got it.
Now you try.
SQUIGGLE POWER ACTIVATE!!!
Ha ha ha hoooo!
You're supposed to squiggle, NOT WIGGLE, Johnny Boo!
WIGGLE
WIGGLE
WIGGLE

CHAPTER SIX:

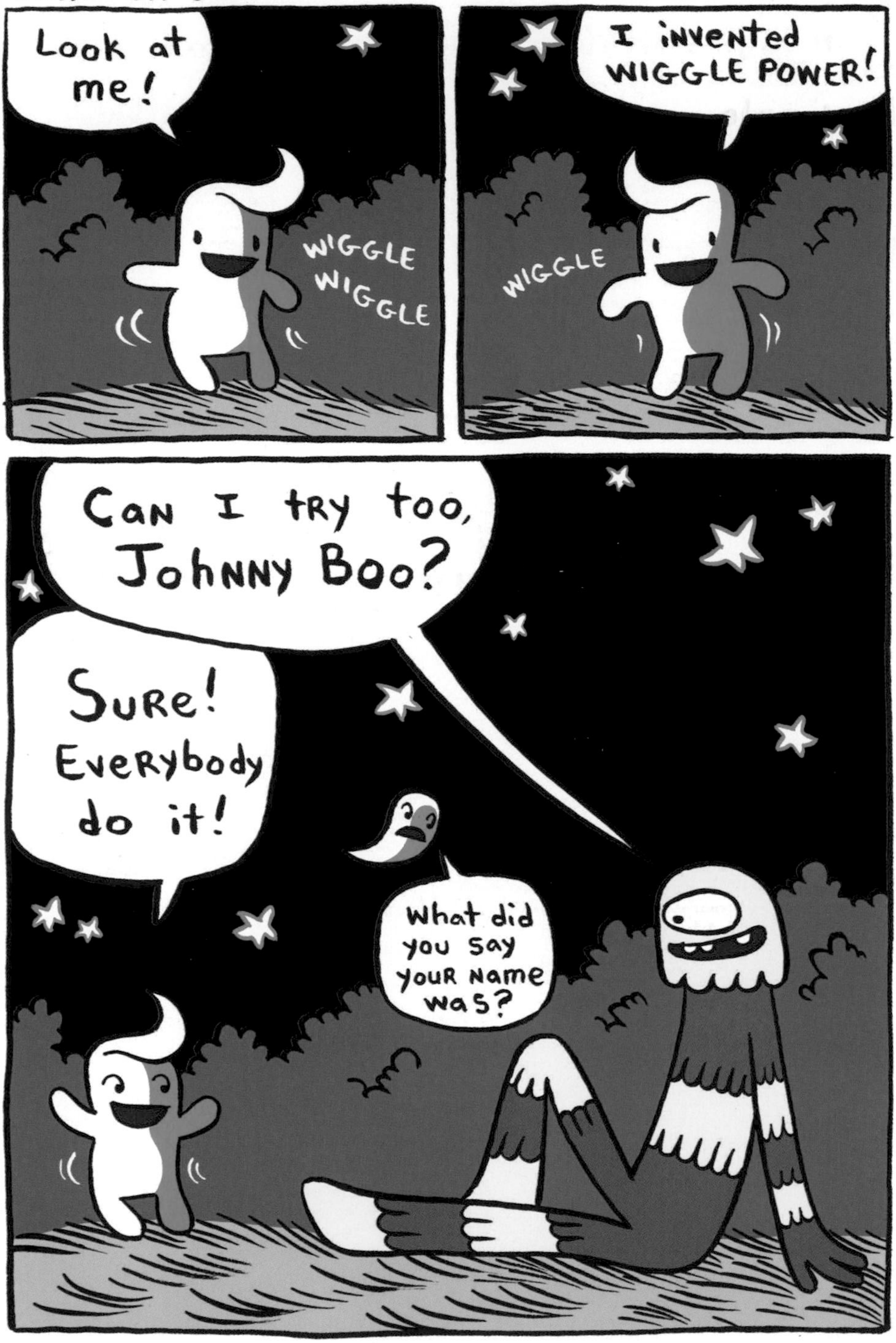
Look at me!
WIGGLE WIGGLE
I invented WIGGLE POWER!
WIGGLE
Can I try too, Johnny Boo?
Sure! Everybody do it!
What did you say your name was?

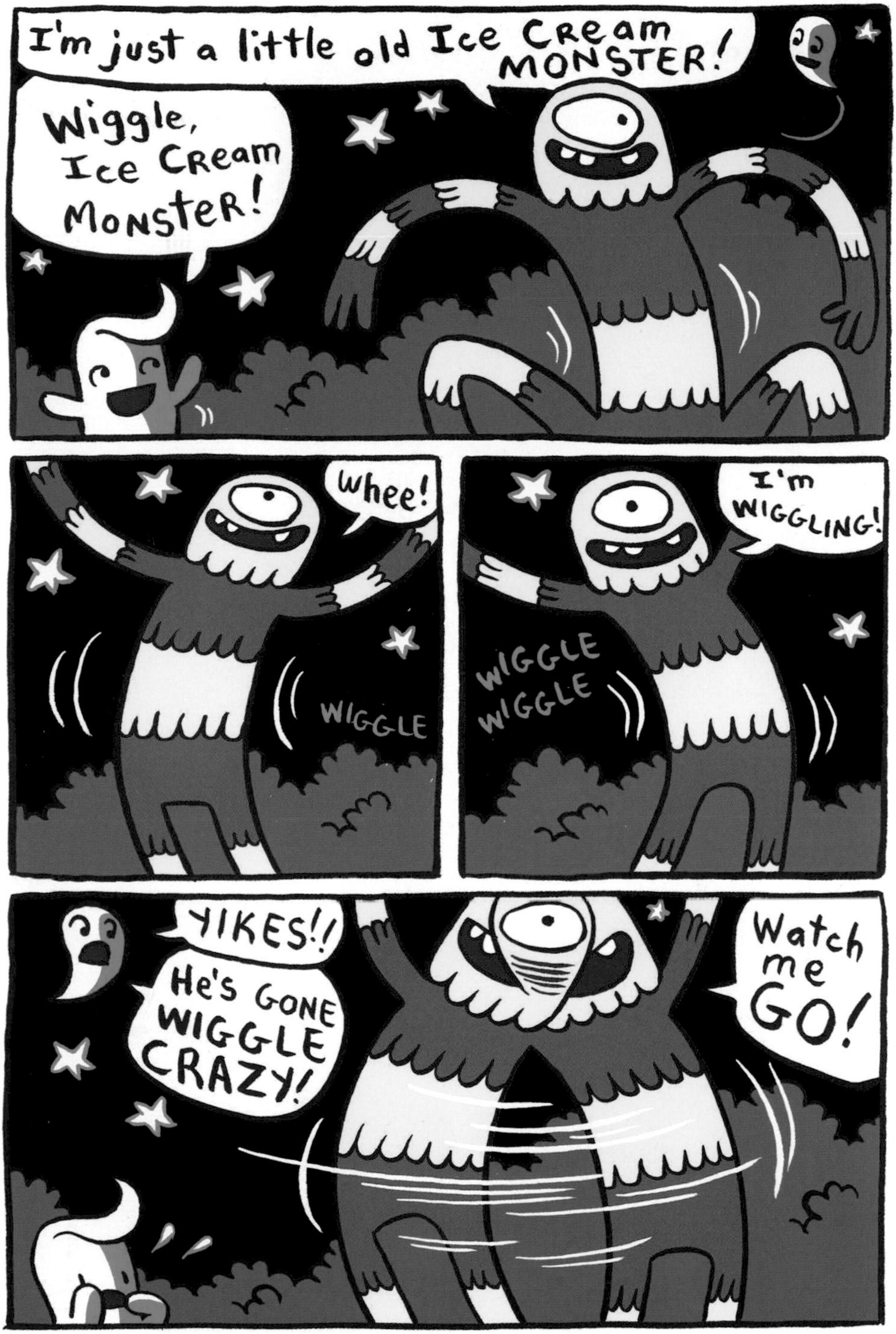
I'm just a little old Ice Cream MONSTER!
Wiggle, Ice Cream Monster!
Whee!
WIGGLE
I'm WIGGLING!
WIGGLE WIGGLE
YIKES!!
He's GONE WIGGLE CRAZY!
Watch me GO!

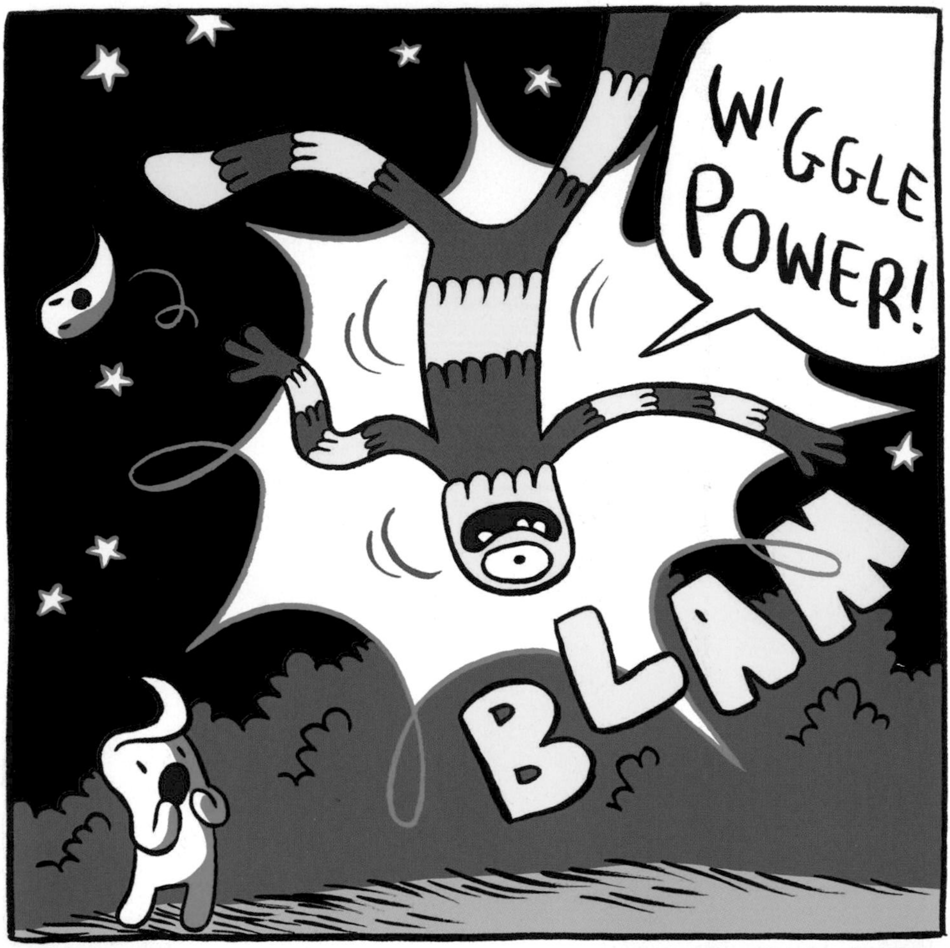
WIGGLE POWER!
BLAM

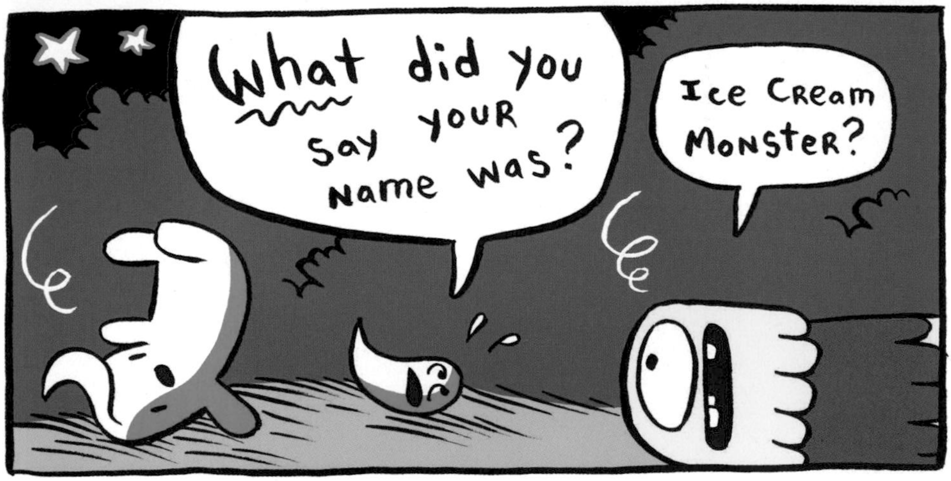
What did you say your name was?
Ice Cream Monster?

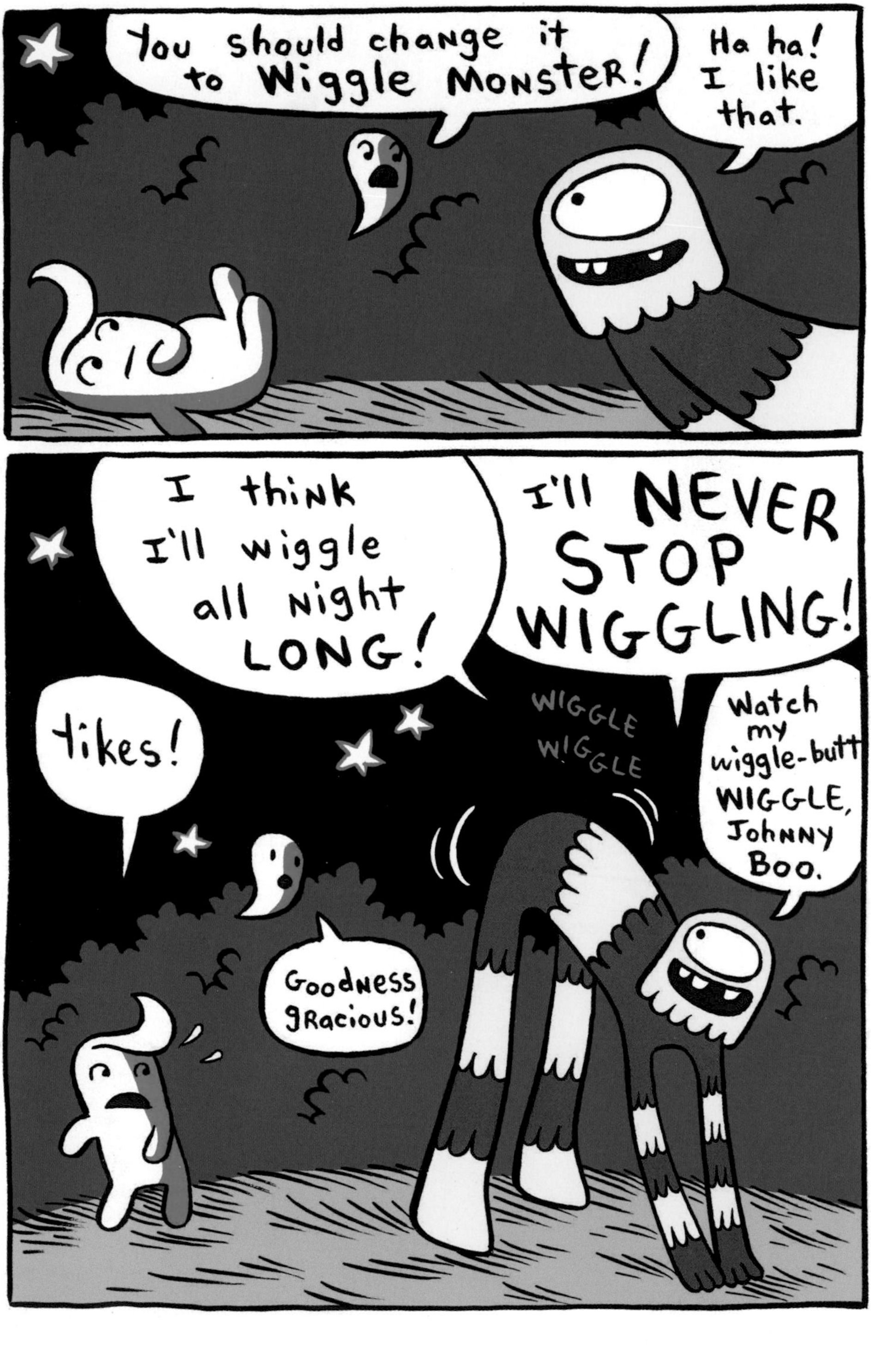
You should change it to Wiggle Monster!
Ha ha! I like that.
I think I'll wiggle all night LONG!
I'll NEVER STOP WIGGLING!
Yikes!
WIGGLE WIGGLE
Watch my wiggle-butt WIGGLE, Johnny Boo.
Goodness gracious!

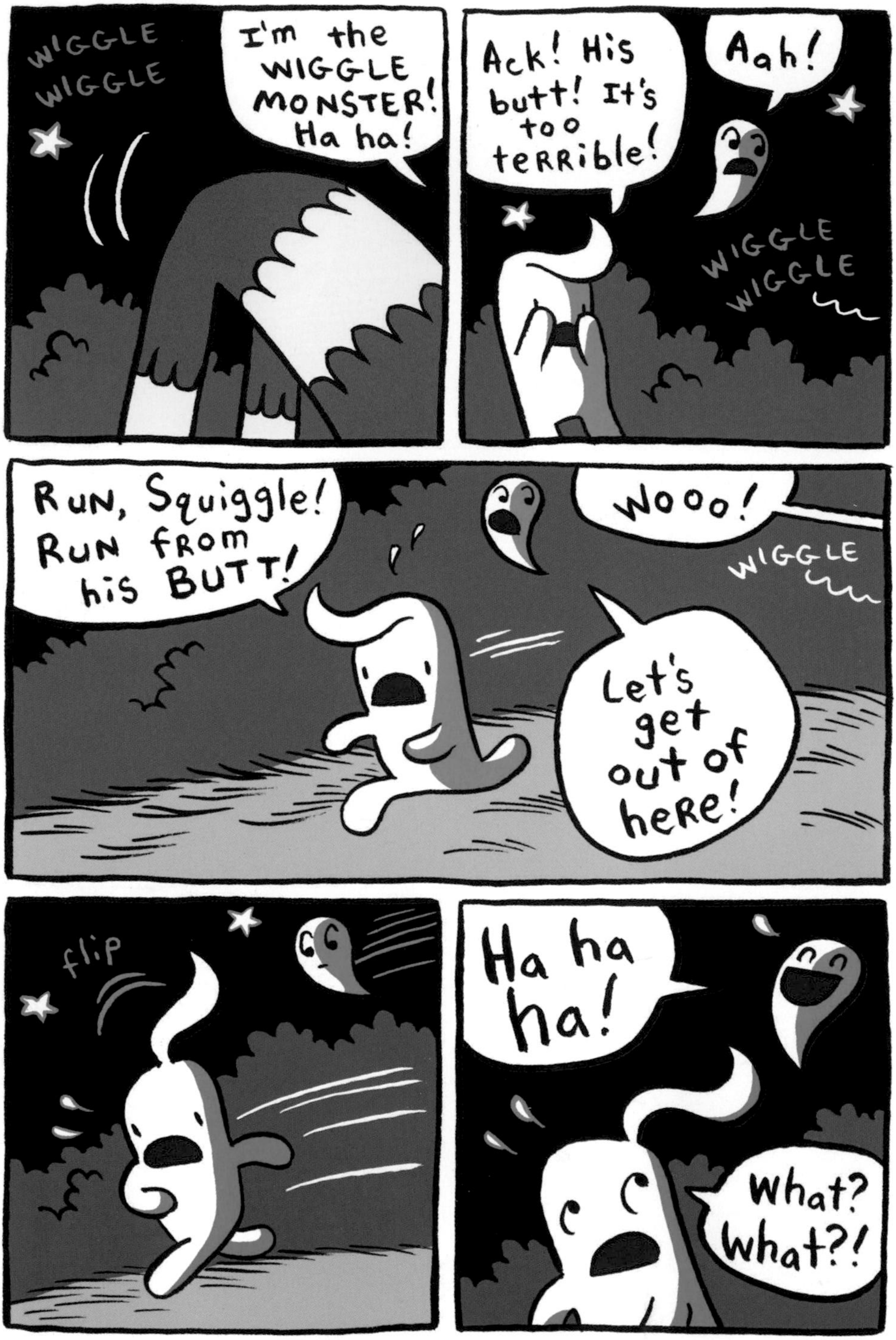

WIGGLE
WIGGLE
I'm the WIGGLE MONSTER! Ha ha!
Ack! His butt! It's too terrible!
Aah!
WIGGLE
WIGGLE
RUN, Squiggle! RUN FROM his BUTT!
Wooo!
WIGGLE
Let's get out of here!
flip
Ha ha ha!
What? What?!

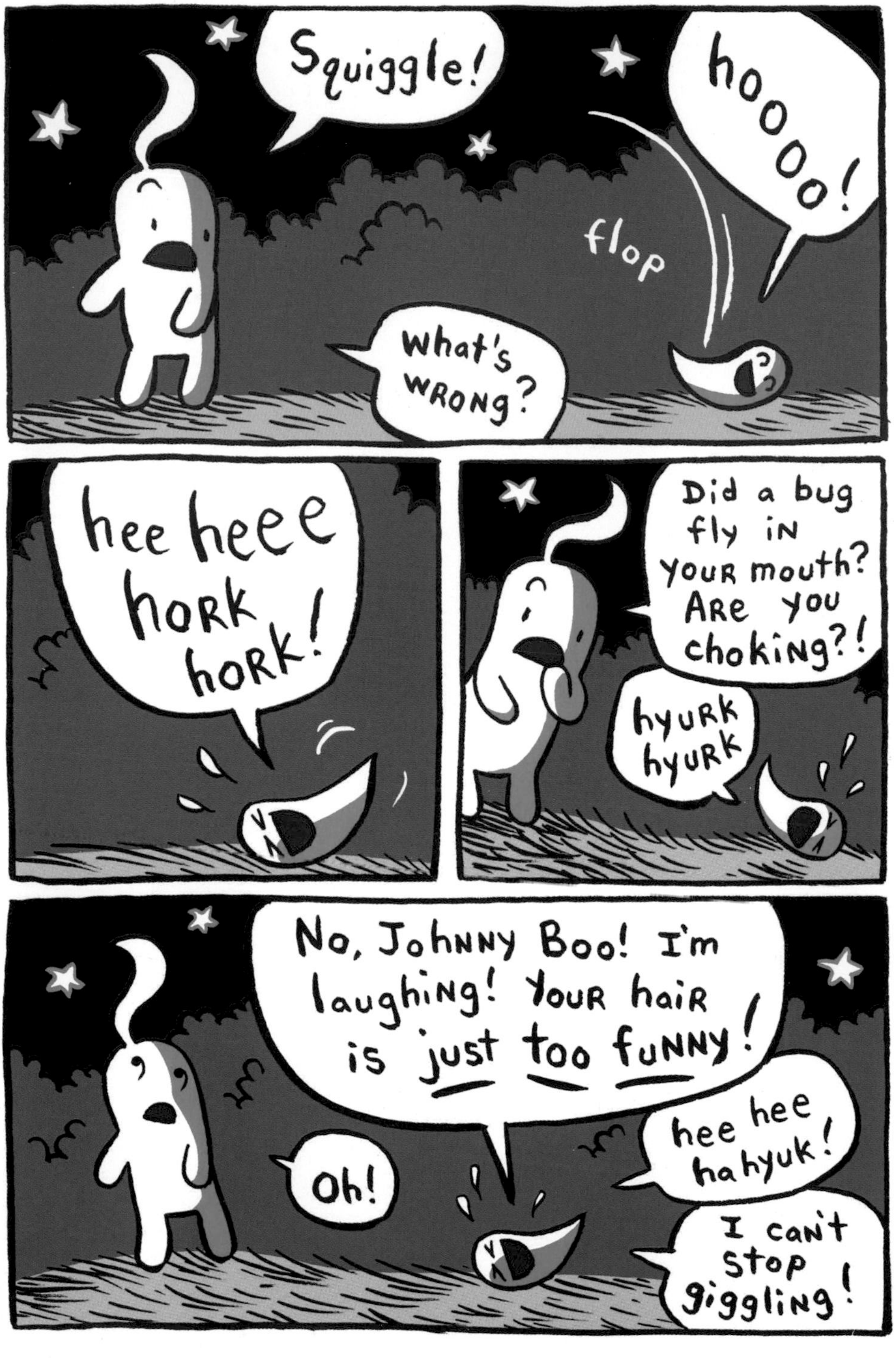
Squiggle!
hooooo!
flop
What's WRONG?
hee heee hork hork!
Did a bug fly in your mouth? Are you choking?!
hyurk hyurk
No, Johnny Boo! I'm laughing! Your hair is just too funny!
Oh!
hee hee hahyuk!
I can't stop giggling!

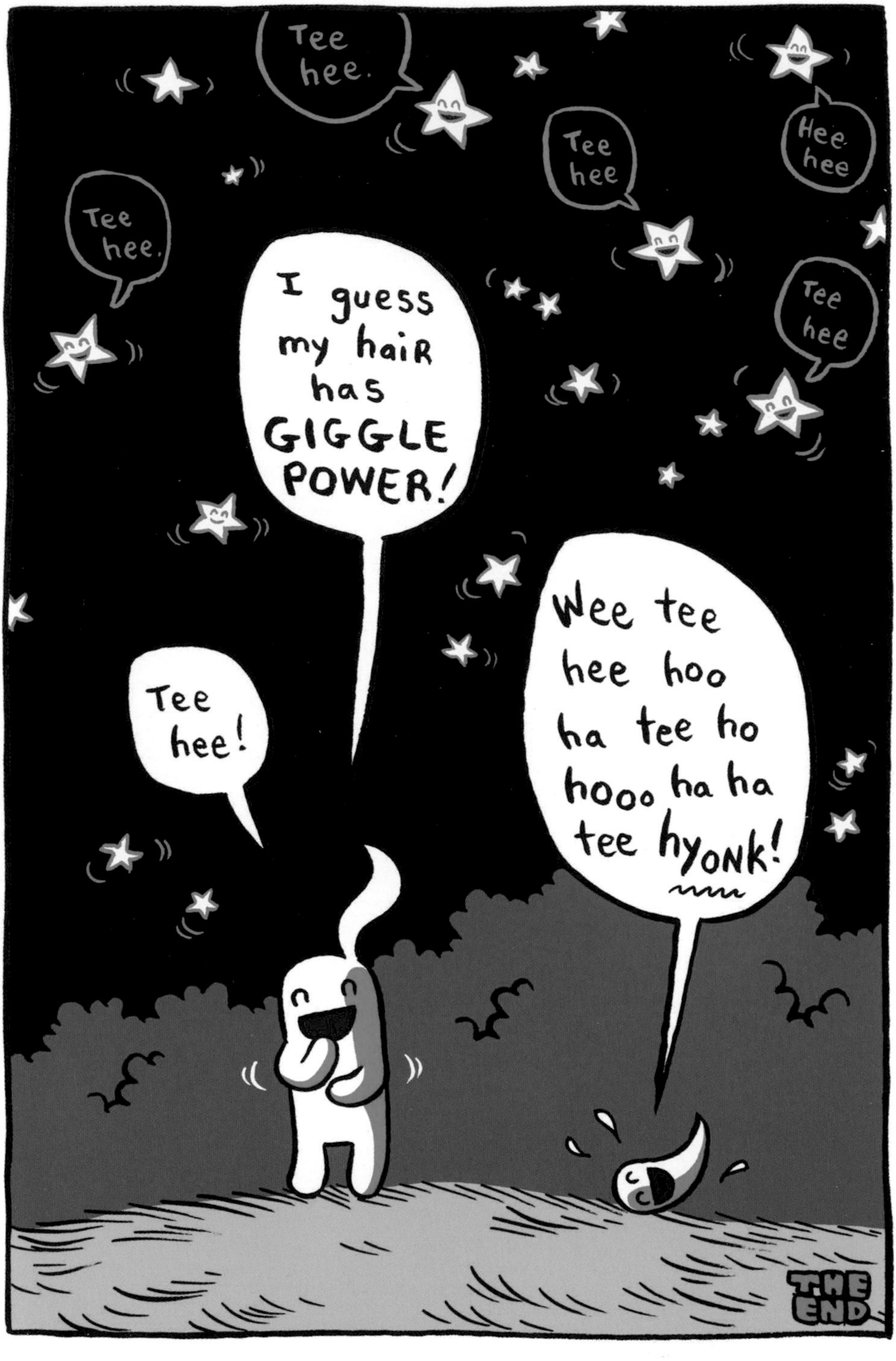
Tee hee.
Tee hee
Hee hee
Tee hee.
Tee hee
I guess my hair has GIGGLE POWER!
Tee hee!
Wee tee hee hoo ha tee ho hooo ha ha tee hyONK!
THE END

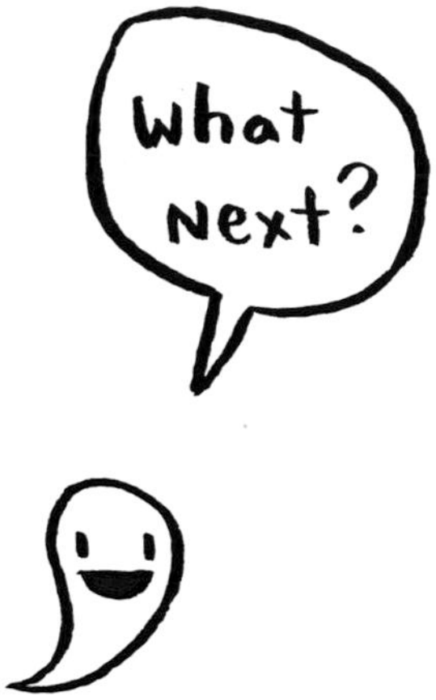
What next?

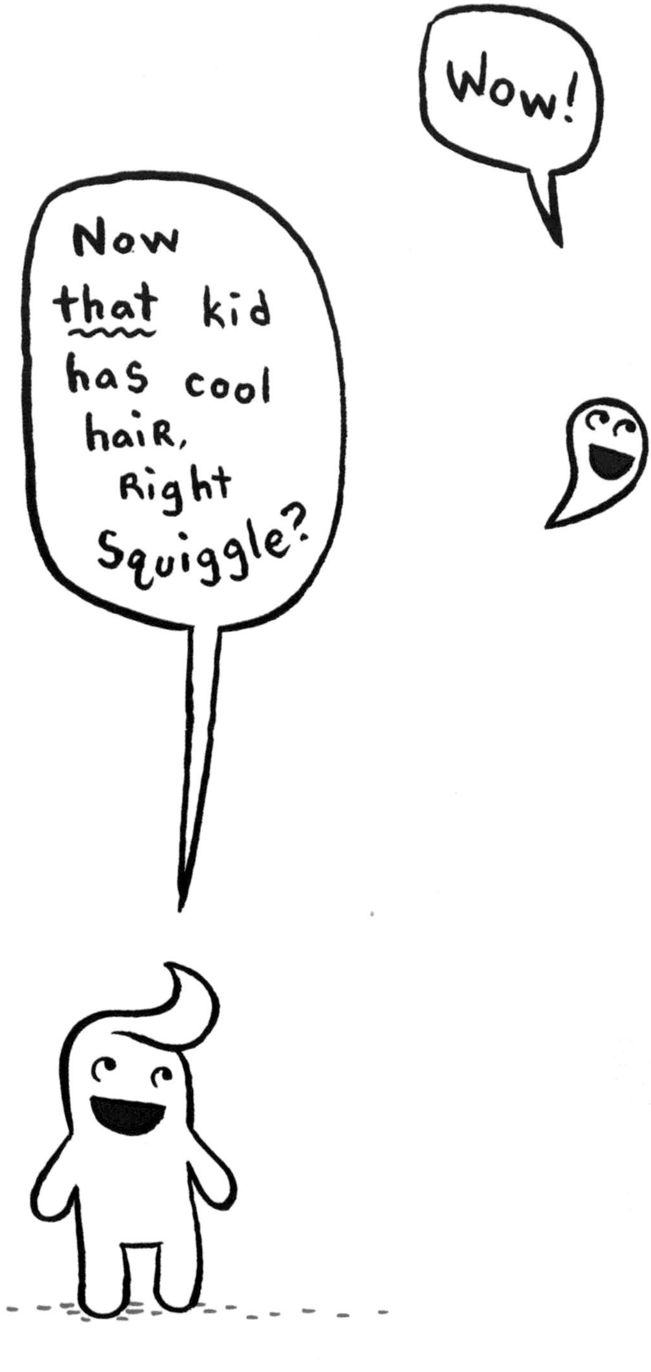
Wow!
Now that kid has cool hair, Right Squiggle?

A PHOTO OF THE AUTHOR AS A YOUNG MAN: